D0333123

Ab... ...shi.

THE INVENTORY
WINTER STORM

Aberdeenshire

3220405

Also by Andy Briggs:

The Inventory: Iron Fist

The Inventory: Gravity

The Inventory: Black Knight

THE INVENTORY

WINTER STORM

ANDY BRIGGS

SCHOLASTIC

Scholastic Children's Books
An imprint of Scholastic Ltd
Euston House, 24 Eversholt Street, London, NW1 1DB, UK
Registered office: Westfield Road, Southam, Warwickshire, CV47 0RA
SCHOLASTIC and associated logos are trademarks and/or
registered trademarks of Scholastic Inc.

First published in the UK by Scholastic Ltd, 2018

Text copyright © Andy Briggs, 2018

The right of Andy Briggs to be identified as the author
of this work has been asserted by him

ISBN 978 1407 16205 8

A CIP catalogue record for this book
is available from the British Library.

All rights reserved.
This book is sold subject to the condition that it shall not,
by way of trade or otherwise, be lent, hired out or otherwise circulated in
any form of binding or cover other than that in which it is published. No
part of this publication may be reproduced, stored in a retrieval system,
or transmitted in any form or by any means (electronic, mechanical,
photocopying, recording or otherwise) without prior
written permission of Scholastic Limited.

Printed by CPI Group (UK) Ltd, Croydon, CR0 4YY
Papers used by Scholastic Children's Books are made
from wood grown in sustainable forests.

1 3 5 7 9 10 8 6 4 2

This is a work of fiction. Names, characters, places, incidents
and dialogues are products of the author's imagination or are used
fictitiously. Any resemblance to actual people, living or dead,
events or locales is entirely coincidental.

www.scholastic.co.uk

CLOSING THE DOORS
ON THE INVENTORY'S BIGGEST SECRET:

DAVID STEVENS AND LINAS ALSENAS –
YOU GUYS ROCK!

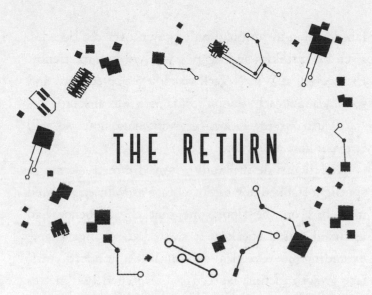

THE RETURN

"Revolutions start with the tiniest of moments." Onslow Winter stopped pacing the stage, extended his arms — then slowly drew them together until his index fingers were touching. It was a touch of showmanship the technological genius had brought to every presentation over many years. "And we have the most *awesome* small there is!"

The thousand-strong crowd of technology journalists leaned forward in rapt anticipation like the star-struck fans they were. From the moment Winter had become a telecoms billionaire with the launch of his revolutionary mobile phone, he had been a technology superhero, and fan devotion to him had only grown over the decades. Even his wrinkles and saggy jowls had become trendy. Every event at Winter Tech was like a pop concert, and secrecy about each new project launch was absolute.

"With our revolutionary nanotechnology, we will reinvent how we invent!"

The lights in the auditorium dimmed. A single spotlight stabbed down centre stage as Winter gestured to a box on the floor, one that the audience had assumed was a speaker. It started to change shape, extending into a vertical column like a hundred years' tree growth in time-lapse. As it stretched two metres tall, the audience oohed in appreciation, then burst into applause. Winter waved his hand to encourage them to keep going.

"Nanobots. You've all heard of them before. Some of you have seen them. Tiny mechanical robots that can work together for a greater task. But these..." He paused for a moment to admire the black monolith that had formed onstage. It was so matt black that it seemed to suck the illumination from the spotlights pointed at it. "These are something else. They are not tiny robots. No. What you are looking at are the first *bio-bots*. Like you, like me, this column is built of *living* components, each a millimetre long, that have been engineered into a programmable living swarm."

You could have heard a pin drop in the auditorium as the assembled crowd tried to work out what he meant. That was the trouble with being Onslow Winter: his mind worked far ahead of most people's. The corners of his mouth twisted into a smile as gasps of astonishment slowly rippled through the crowd as the audience began to understand.

"It's something more than a robot or a cyborg. Capable of adapting to its environment and shaping itself with almost limitless possibilities! It's a living bioborg. I call it *Winter Storm*."

With that, the smooth monolith suddenly whirled like a tornado, with a sound like a billion marbles clattering together, before finally taking the shape of a towering arm that pivoted and waved at the crowd. By now the applause was deafening. People had taken to stomping their feet on the floor in admiration.

Still the whirlwind turned – and the resulting construction made everybody freeze in silence. It was a seven-foot-tall humanoid. A matt-black robot formed of smooth contours. The head was in the shape of a sleek futuristic biker's helmet. Although it was featureless, people felt their skin prickle as the head turned side to side to study them. The lack of eyes didn't mean they couldn't feel the living machine's gaze bore into them.

With a soft clump that sounded like it was walking on bubble wrap, the humanoid stepped forward – then raised its fist in triumph.

On cue, the crowd went wild with cheers and thunderous clapping. The applause was so loud that it almost drowned out the explosion above them.

A circular section of ceiling blew away in a shower of smoke and plaster dust. People began scrambling for the exits, only to find them blocked by menacing thugs wearing body armour, their faces concealed behind black plastic shields like hockey masks. They wielded peculiar rifles with a white central chamber from which a faint mist steadily poured. With a twitch of the trigger, one of the men shot a blast of frigid air across those nearest him, immediately encasing them in ice.

"Do not panic," boomed a voice from above, and a figure slowly descended from the hole in the roof. There was a faint whirl from the antigravity boots he wore as they carried him to the stage, where a shocked Winter stood. "You will not be harmed."

The frozen people suddenly shattered into countless

ice shards. The villain sighed and gestured to the broken pieces.

"Correction. Nobody *else* will be harmed if you just cooperate."

Onslow Winter was nothing if not a performer. With the frightened eyes of hundreds of people on him, he raised himself to his full height and approached the newcomer. Behind him, the Winter Storm humanoid mirrored his stance, acting as a towering bodyguard. Winter stared at the figure's eyes, which were white, with no pupils. They were unnerving, to say the least.

"Onslow Winter, I am here for your wonderful Winter Storm." The newcomer gestured to the humanoid. "Hand it over, or I will freeze your adoring fans, one by one." He gestured to the audience.

Winter licked his dry lips and finally found his voice.

"Wh-who are you?"

"I am your biggest fan." The figure's smile was absent of humour. "But you may call me the Collector."

CUT AND PASTE

It was far colder than Dev thought it should be. Goosebumps broke out across his arms, and his breath fogged the air in front of him. There was an unusual metallic taste to the air, and the room was so quiet that he could hear his blood pounding in his ears.

But these were the just minor details he was focusing on, because he was trying not to accept what he was seeing with his own eyes. He, Lot and Karl Tyker had just walked through a room with cryogenic pods hanging from the ceiling. An unidentified woman had been in one of the pods, in suspended animation.

And now they were going further into the ultra-secret

Black Zone of the Inventory, and Dev wasn't sure if he was ready to face whatever might be there.

"Keep calm," said a voice inside his head. It wasn't his; it belonged to Tyker, who was leading the way just ahead. Tyker had spoken using the TelePath device that Dev had given him. It allowed the wearer to communicate telepathically with others nearby, but this little unit also held Tyker's saved memories from a previous life. A life Tyker had lived over a hundred years ago, before he too was placed in suspended animation in the Inventory's chilly Black Zone, where that unknown woman now lay.

"This is weird," whispered Lot from behind Dev. She hadn't heard Tyker's message, but Dev was impressed with how calm she was. In school he had always been too shy to even speak to the girl with infectious smile, until he had accidentally turned up at her birthday party. Since then they had travelled the world, battled incredible dangers and become firm friends. Or could it be something more than just friends, he wondered. . .

"What's in there?" Lot said, breaking his thoughts.

Ahead was an aisle of twenty cylinders made from thick reinforced glass, each two metres tall. Brass caps and panels attached to the glass and connected to an array of tubes. Heavy condensation hid the contents from view. He had seen something similar – cloning pods used to create new life – in the Inventory's Red Zone. That's the area where the most destructive or sensitive items were held – or so Dev had thought, until he discovered the existence of the Black Zone. The pods he was looking at now were almost certainly larger versions. He steeled himself for what he might find inside.

Lot had already stepped ahead and wiped the condensation from the nearest cylinder. Dev heard her sharp intake of breath and knew, even though she blocked his view, what she saw. With a trembling hand, Dev reached out and put a hand on her shoulder and slowly pulled her back – revealing the slumbering face beyond the glass.

It was his own.

Dev had known he was a clone created by his uncle, the Inventory's curator, Charles Parker. He was – in a twisted artificial family tree – related to the monstrous Shadow Helix villains known as the Collector and Kardach, who were products of his uncle's high-tech, Frankensteinian experiments. In fact, that made Charles Parker more his father than uncle, although he acted like neither.

But seeing an exact duplicate of himself suspended in a milky fluid felt oddly reassuring. It felt somehow natural, as if he had seen this before, perhaps in a dream. Although he was embarrassed to think the clone was naked; luckily the liquid was cloudy enough to block the view . . . further down.

"What is going on?" asked Lot in a small voice. Before Dev could stop her, she darted across to another pod and wiped away the veil of water droplets. Sure enough, another exact duplicate of Dev floated inside. She turned and stared at him, uncomprehending.

"Clones," Dev said with a shrug. What else could he say?

"I thought that meant, you know, they made one of you and that was that!" Lot exclaimed, looking at the other pods. "This is . . . this is . . . *weird*. And I have seen plenty of strange stuff these past few months! *Plenty!*"

"I don't fully understand it myself," Dev said. Why had somebody cut-and-pasted him into liquid vats deep underground? "I'm as confused as you are. More so!"

They both turned their gaze on Tyker, who had stood silently to the side.

"I bet *you* know," said Dev. Then he pointed at the TelePath behind Tyker's ear. "Especially as you're regaining your memories. You know what this is, don't you?"

Tyker nodded, but avoided looking either Dev or Lot in the eye. "Yes. I helped build the Inventory. And, as you know —" he jerked a thumb towards the cryo-pods in the room next door "— I was brought in and out of suspended animation by your uncle, and others, as they required my services."

"So you and the others back there — they just defrost you when they need you? You're like a walking, talking ice lolly."

Tyker sighed. "It seems so." He gestured to the clone tanks. "These are something I had no part of. They're clones of you. Obviously. Created at the same time. Waiting to be activated."

"Activated?" Dev echoed uncertainly.

Tyker stepped forward and gently took Dev's wrist. Then he pulled back Dev's sleeve, revealing his bare forearm.

"Look at those scars," Tyker said, turning Dev's arm so Lot could see.

"He doesn't have any," she said.

"Exactly. What about you?"

Lot frowned and rolled back her own sleeve. There

were several tiny scars. Some she had gained while enjoying various extreme sports with her parents, but many others were from the myriad dangers she had been through with Dev and Mason. Countless dings, cuts and bruises that had almost faded over time.

Tyker released Dev's wrist. "And just how many times have you suffered drastic injuries?"

Dev shrugged. "I've had broken bones and stuff," he said vaguely. "Eema puts me into a machine that puts me to sleep and patches me up. It can fix bones – anything, really."

Tyker nodded. "Does she? Perhaps that's what you are told."

Dev shook his head, not quite understanding. Tyker placed a hand on Dev's head.

"Or do they suck out your personality and –" he moved his hand and tapped Lot on the head "– drop it in a brand-new body?"

Dev involuntarily stepped back in surprise, his head turning between Tyker and the clones. "No." The word barely made it past his lips. "That can't be true."

Tyker walked between the pods. "Think about it. How many times should you have died, Dev? With your synaesthesia, you are far too valuable to be sent on missions where you could die, just like that." He snapped his fingers to emphasize the point.

Dev moved closer to a pod so he could examine his clone more closely. It looked as if it was peacefully sleeping. An array of fine tubes connected to its body in multiple places, feeding the clone and keeping it alive. On impulse, Dev leaned closer and tapped on the glass.

The clone's eyes popped open and stared straight back at him. Dev leapt back in shock as the clone began to violently thrash in the liquid. It opened its mouth to scream and immediately took in the fluid around it. Dev could only watch as the clone pounded against the glass, silently pleading to be released. Its body jerked as it began to drown.

A blue ink suddenly injected into the tank. The clone fell limp, eyes rolling closed. Dev shivered; it was as if he'd almost witnessed his own death. Only the gentle rising of the clone's chest assured him otherwise.

MARRAKECH

"Oh, come on, Dev, let me have a go this time," Lot pleaded. "You promised!"

With no missions, and Dev's uncle and Sergeant Wade away on World Consortium business, Dev and Lot had sneaked into the Red Zone at the lowest level of the Inventory. It was the most heavily secured area, where the most dangerous inventions were stored, including Dev's favourite: the Iron Fist gauntlet, which created a giant mech battle suit around the wearer. Being a killjoy, his uncle hadn't allowed him to use it for a while, even for missions, telling him it was too dangerous.

Nobody else was able to remove it from the Inventory, but that wasn't a problem for Dev. He was a living security key, which meant he was the only person in the Inventory who could take technology outside. So for four days they had taken the gauntlet to the surface, where a fake farm had been constructed over the Inventory entrance as cover, including a farmhouse – where Dev lived with his uncle – and several barns, complete with animatronic animals to appease any curious visitors. The back of the barns had provided the perfect cover from any technicians who happened to wander by.

Dev stepped from the mech as the tiny, blue metal plates collapsed around him and folded almost impossibly back into the heavy gauntlet. He looked around the improvised assault course they had made from hay bales and old farm machinery.

A tractor still smouldered from when he had got a little too carried away using the mech's laser cannons.

Lot held out her hands expectantly.

"OK," said Dev, feeling a surprising twang of jealousy that somebody else was about to use his toy. He was about to hand it over when the alarm sounded on their phones with a message alert: an artefact had been detected. The Inventory's robotic guardian, Eema, demanded the team assemble immediately.

With no time to return the gauntlet to the Red Zone, Dev and Lot hid it under some hay in the barn and hurried to meet the others. Dev's uncle would go berserk if he knew that something so precious had been taken out of the Inventory, let alone so clumsily hidden, but Dev knew he'd be back soon and would show Lot how to use it then.

"This is going to be brilliant!" cried Mason.

Seated behind him in the floating Avrocar, Aaron tried not to chuckle when Riya rolled her eyes. Dev and Lot sat beside Mason in silence, focused on the mission.

Dev, Lot, Mason, Aaron and Riya – the Scavengers, as they were known informally at the Inventory – had been helping catalogue items that were slowly trickling back into the Inventory's shelves. Amongst them: the quake-cancellation device that actually shook the ground so severely it caused a bigger earthquake than the one it was trying to stop; the Hurricane Engine, which could suck in and compress the air before unleashing it with a hurricane punch; and Mason's favourite, the

Internal Balloon – a hot-air balloon that people rode *inside* of. They reached their destination by plummeting to earth and bouncing. At least in theory.

These were mostly items stolen from the Collector's raid on the Inventory and had subsequently been recovered from various sites around the globe by World Consortium tracking teams. Cataloguing proved to be a pleasant enough task with the Inventory's technicians – normal people who lived in the town above, who performed a far-from-normal job. The eldest technician, a man called Norman, always took time to joke with them. And everyone, but especially the Scavengers, was watched over by Eema.

The massive spherical robot had rolled through the site, her holographic head popping up with a cheery smiley emoji to whomever she greeted.

"She looks happier than usual," Lot had said to Dev. "I wonder if she's had some reprogramming?"

Dev, on the other hand, had been more subdued with the others ever since the Black Knight incident. It had been the first time they had lost a team member, Wan-Soo. He had been a traitor, it turned out, but his death had affected Dev deeply. Every night before falling asleep, he had replayed the events in his mind, certain there was something not quite right about how it all went down.

And despite being surrounded by the world's greatest technology, the team had become restless. Mason had even started to miss school.

"That's just crazy talk," Aaron had told him. "You've got cabin fever!"

A new mission was exactly what they had needed.

Lot's voice brought Dev back to the present. "Cloaking shield activated," she said, glancing at the liquid control panel in front of them. "At least nobody will see us coming."

Outside the disc-shaped Avrocar, the bottom of the hull was covered with a giant display screen that projected the image of the starry sky above them. From the ground, they were invisible.

"Just as well," said Mason, gazing out of the panoramic viewing screen.

Below them was a vast night-time market square of Jemaa el-Fnaa, the whole area alive with lights and packed with thousands of people. From there, a warren of narrow streets and covered markets ran for kilometres within the ancient walled medina of Marrakech.

The Avro hovered in position above the square.

With such a densely packed space, there was nowhere to land, not even the irregular roofs of the surrounding buildings.

Dev pulled the buckles on his boots tight. "Activate your Absorb-o-Boots."

Small blue LEDs in the ankles of the knee-high boots blinked to indicate the devices were working. The Avro's ramp opened as the aircraft positioned as closely as the autopilot darted to a rooftop on the edge of the square, narrowly avoiding a nest of television aerials and satellite dishes.

Dev led the way to the edge of the ramp. In the past, his fear of heights would have had his knees trembling, but since starting his duties in the Inventory he had been on top of the tallest tower in Canada, flown in an armoured suit, jumped from an aeroplane without a parachute and even been into space. After all that, it would require a huge effort to remain scared of heights.

"Don't forget to deactivate once we're on the ground," he reminded them. "Let's go!"

Dev jumped the ten metres to the rooftop below. He landed on both feet, the Absorb-o-Boots taking the impact so it felt as if he was landing on a soft bed. Without hesitation he jumped again, the three storeys down into the shadowy edge of the square where there were only a few people milling around.

The rest of the team followed, Riya performing an elegant somersault just before landing.

"Show-off!" Mason grinned as he stumbled with his awkward landing.

A few tourists who had seen them jump down looked around briefly, mystified, but then resumed their slow shuffling through the crowd.

Dev pulled out his phone. It was far beyond any technology available to buy on the high street, capable of holographic displays and communication underground, but in this instance, it had a simple flat display with Eema's animated head peering out above a map of the medina, complete with a tiny animated mouth as she spoke:

"All right, team, the tech has been detected in the north-west area of the souk. Be careful; from the energy signature, we suspect it may be a weapon of some sort."

They had all heard the message via tiny earpieces, so they wordlessly followed Dev as he led the way in the direction marked on his map. They were instantly surrounded by a wall of people who were selling anything you could imagine, from fake watches to fruits and carpets. Luckily, as adolescents, they were ignored by most of the Berber traders, who instead focused on the money-carrying adults.

The air was thick with rich aromas of perfumes, spices and meats made all the more potent by the heat being released by the surrounding desert, back to the star-filled sky. Mason's eyes were wide with delight as they passed stalls of exotic fruits and foods which he had never seen before. "Is that a sheep's head?" he asked with a mix of awe and disgust, pointing to one stall.

Riya grinned, feeling at home in the bustling market, which reminded her of the Brazilian slums where she had been raised. "Yup, and that's its brain next to it." She pointed to a white bumpy mass on a separate stand and was delighted to see Mason blanch in disgust.

The Scavengers had to shoulder their way through the crowd, a massive mix of cultures from around the world, from Asia to America, Africa and across Europe. Dev thought if he closed his eyes he could probably hear every language on Earth, all in one place.

"WOW!" hissed Mason as they passed a knot of people surrounding a snake charmer, who was kneeling on a mat playing a rhythmic tune to a hooded cobra, which swayed hypnotically, much to the amusement of the crowd.

A boy who had a young Barbary ape on his shoulder attempted to put it on Lot's own shoulder. "Go away," she growled, then muttered, "That's so cruel."

Despite his mood, Dev couldn't stop smiling. Lot was one tough cookie.

They reached the entrance to the souk. It was nothing more than a narrow street with countless stalls either side selling everything from *babouches* to handbags, from cheap souvenirs to silver trinkets.

Electric lights were strung from a covering overhead, woven around numerous hanging Arabian lanterns and tinkling Berber charms. Dev checked his phone.

"This is the way."

For several minutes they pushed through the crowds, which gave no sign of thinning out. Every time they reached a junction, Dev diligently followed Eema's directions on his phone until they stepped from the covered street into a small open-air square filled with fruit stands. Aaron pointed at a watermelon that was almost the size of his body.

"That's awesome!"

Riya looked quizzically at him. "Really? You work with the world's best tech and you think a big watermelon is *awesome*?"

"Well, it is," he mumbled.

"We're close," Dev said, peering at his phone. He held it up, slowly circling so they could get a better lock on the signal. He finally settled on another souk branching from the square. "This way. Keep your eyes peeled."

This street felt the same as the others, except the stalls appeared to trade more mechanical items. One sold a range of balancing scales and silver plates, while another was filled with parts for motor engines. The crowds were just as relentless, this time with the added nuisance of scooters weaving through at high speeds. Several times the team members had to dart aside at the buzzing sound of a two-stroke engine.

Dev stopped to look at a stall filled with old cine cameras. Some were large and bulky; other Super 8 cameras looked more like guns with a wide lens instead of a barrel. They were all scuffed with age, some stained with desert sand; the paint on their focus numbers and text of the various switches had faded with age. The range was overwhelming, and he was sure they would fetch a high price back home.

"We're not sightseeing," said Lot, nudging him.

"No, this is it. It's here somewhere."

"You want to buy?" said the trader, emerging from

the shadows of his stall. He was a Berber, his dark face creased from the sun.

"Just looking," said Dev with a smile.

The trader pulled a small camera at random. "This is antique. They filmed *Lawrence of Arabia* with this. You buy?"

"Lawrence of what?" whispered Mason.

Dev shook his head. "No idea." He held up his hand to the trader. "No, just looking. The only problem is we don't know what for."

Then something caught his eye. It looked like a slightly larger cine camera but, unlike the others, it looked new. The lens was far too big, and there weren't any numbers or markings on the device.

His examination of the camera was interrupted by a rising wave of screams from further down the souk. Dev, Lot and Mason instinctively stood closer together; their ears were well-attuned for yells of panic. Riya and Aaron craned their necks to see the cause of the commotion.

Then a seven-foot-tall matt-black figure strode into view. The top of its featureless head cracked against a low souk roof, smashing dangling lanterns aside.

Behind walked the Collector. Riya and Aaron had

never met the fiend before, but Dev, Lot and Mason were all too familiar with him.

"Ah, the merry band of thieves," said the Collector, standing in front of his huge guardian. "Always here to be irksome."

"Scavengers," Mason corrected him. "We didn't nick this stuff in the first place."

The Collector waved his hand dismissively. "Alas for you, I have no time for distractions." He indicated to Dev. "Winter Storm. Annihilate."

Dev watched in astonishment as the large figure suddenly crumbled to black dust that took to the air and swarmed with the sound of angry bees. The peculiar cloud bore down on him like a vengeful sandstorm.

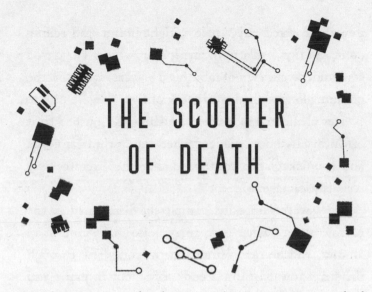

THE SCOOTER
OF DEATH

Dev's response to the threat was instinctive. He snatched the device from the stall while at the same time his synaesthesia surged into action, reversing the actuators on his Absorb-o-Boots. He stomped the ground and the boots propelled him into the air in a superhuman leap.

He glimpsed Lot and the others leaping aside to avoid the bio-bots as they swooped beneath him, just missing him.

Then he lost sight of them all as he sailed halfway along the narrow street – which suddenly was covered again with wooden roofs. Seconds later he came crashing down, the timber splintering on impact. Dev tumbled into the covered street below, right into a stall selling dates and figs – splattering fruit everywhere. The dazed stallholder yelled in Arabic as Dev crumpled to the ground, along with an avalanche of figs.

Dev clambered to his feet, brushing the mushed fruit off him. His boots made a wheezing, asthmatic noise, and a quick glance confirmed that the circuitry was seriously damaged.

Dev swayed uneasily, completely disoriented in the narrow street. Then a rushing noise made him snap around, and he saw Winter Storm corkscrew through the street towards him. People cried out in panic and leapt from its path.

Dev pulled the artefact close to his chest and ran in the opposite direction as fast as he could.

"Move! Move! Out of my way!" he yelled, shouldering people aside. At first they were reluctant to move, but when they saw the dark cloud behind him, they quickly threw themselves out of the way.

Ahead the street curved and branched into a T-junction. Dev had no idea which way he was heading, but took the sharp left turn in the hope of throwing the nanocloud off his trail. His moment of triumph was short-lived, as the swarm quickly followed. He made a mental note that tricks like that only worked in cartoons.

The dry heat sapped his strength and made running tiresome. Ahead was another junction, where he took a sharp right into a similar-looking alley, and still the cloud followed behind him.

The piercing toot of a scooter horn sounded to his side. If it wasn't bad enough that he was being chased by a cloud, then some idiot wanted to pass him on a scooter! He ignored the sound, vowing that they would have to run him over to get past.

Still the persistent tooting continued. Dev threw a scowl at the driver – and was surprised to see Lot at the handlebars!

"Jump on!" she ordered.

Dev leapt on to the saddle behind her and threw his hands around her waist just as she accelerated forward. The tiny engine whined like a mosquito and Dev was almost thrown from his seat.

"Hold tight!" Lot yelled as she hunched forward over the handlebars, willing the machine to go faster. Her thumb was permanently on the horn and the crowds parted before them at speed.

Dev glanced behind and saw the swarm was still on

their tail. He turned to warn Lot but got a mouthful of her shoulder-length blonde hair as it whipped his face. She angled the scooter so low to take one corner that Dev's head almost cracked against a stall. The thin, bald rear tyre skidded on the dusty ground and the bike shimmied, threatening to dislodge them. But Lot skilfully maintained control.

The swarm took the corner too late – millions of particles bouncing from the baked mud wall – and tore fist-sized chunks off. People yelled as the swarm rushed through them, ultimately leaving them unharmed. Winter Storm had only one target.

"It's still behind us!" yelled Dev as he risked a look.

"Do something! You're the one with the magic powers!"

Dev hated any reference to his special ability as "magical". It was not unlike synaesthesia, a condition many people suffered from, a mixing of the senses. Some people could taste colour; others saw shapes instead of hearing sounds. And others ... controlled technology with their minds.

His knuckles gripped the camera device in his hand so tightly that they had turned white. Dev forced himself to relax a little – which was not easy while they scraped against a wall as Lot took another corner. His confidence wasn't improved by the cackle of delight he heard from her. She was actually enjoying the reckless drive.

His synaesthesia tickled his fingertips and flowed into the artefact, surging through the components in a way he didn't quite understand. Yet the flow of information back told him how to make the machine work without the necessary knowledge of mechanics or electronics. It was just as natural to him as making his toes wiggle without having to understand complex biology.

He was wrong about the device being a camera. It wasn't a lens on the front but a speaker. He located an e-tag labelling the item as the SonicBoom. "It's some kind of audio gun," he called out to Lot.

"Then use it!" she cried. "And DUCK!" she added with a yelp.

Dev just about obeyed as the scooter shot under a string of electrical cables that had fallen loose, swinging across the street at head height. Any sooner and it would have yanked them off the bike ... or worse.

Dev blindly aimed the SonicBoom behind and willed the artefact to fire as he squeezed the trigger. The weapon vibrated in his hand and a moment later a deep bass heavy boom was emitted. Dev could feel his ribs shake and saw the air ripple as the sound wave rolled behind them.

Windowpanes shattered. People dropped to their knees, clutching their ears in pain. Mud, plaster and concrete trickled from the facades of buildings as cracks ran across them.

Dev's shot hit the swarm head-on. The bio-bots were stopped in their tracks, dispersing in every direction as they hit the invisible wall.

"It worked!" whooped Dev.

Lot skidded the scooter to a halt so she could see behind them. The swarm clattered to the ground, carpeting the street.

"Well done—" she began, but stopped as a ripple surged through the black dust, as if each particle was part of a Mexican wave. Then it began to re-form in the shape of the huge humanoid.

"Not good," stated Dev. "Go! Go!"

Lot squeezed the throttle and they surged forward. Winter Storm had yet to fully complete its transformation into a humanoid before it began running in pursuit. The lower legs were still a swirling mass of particles, but it was gaining on them.

Dev fired again, willing the power to the max. The sound wave that erupted from the device was so fierce it almost jolted the weapon from his hand. The shock wave pushed the bike faster than the straining engine would allow, and Lot struggled for control as the scooter popped into an involuntary wheelie.

Stalls, building facades and the roof of the souk were torn asunder by the audio blast. Before the sonic wave could reach Winter Storm, the swarm suddenly dissipated into smoke. Dev could see the rippling air of the blast travel through the swarm   but the particles then regrouped back into the human shape and continued relentlessly forward.

"They're learning. . ." Dev said, feeling panic rise within him.

Lot struggled to hold the scooter's wheelie, but the machine was never built for such manoeuvres and wobbled precariously. She thrust the front wheel down using all her body weight   before realizing that there was nothing ahead but a white wall with a traditional Moroccan arched wooden door.

The scooter slammed into the door at speed, and it splintered open from the top, acting as a ramp that pitched them into the courtyard beyond. The scooter pivoted through the air – throwing off both Dev and Lot.

The scooter crashed into a wall. Handlebars, wheels and engine fragments shot in every direction.

Lot landed hard on a pile of damp, smelly cow hides, and Dev landed with a splash in a stone pool of a vile-smelling liquid. He thrashed as the liquid burned his skin, his feet slipping on the slick bottom of the vat. They had ended up in a tannery, the air ripe with the smell of ammonia used to turn the cow pelts into soft leather.

Dev heaved himself out of the vat, dripping with a liquid of which the principle ingredient was pigeon poop. His skin stung and the smell was overpowering, yet he still gripped the SonicBoom tightly in his hand.

He risked opening his eyes in time to see Winter Storm bear down on him. A mighty hand coiled around his neck and hoisted him off his feet. Dev choked, clawing at the hand, which felt as cool and smooth as polished stone. His vision faded as he felt the SonicBoom yanked from his grasp. He was aware of Lot shouting, but her voice seemed to come from far away.

Then he lost consciousness and felt as if he was falling into a bottomless black pit...

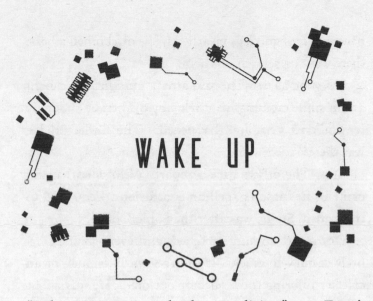

WAKE UP

"Pulse rising, cortisone levels normalizing," came Eema's voice out of the darkness.

Blackness gave way to the blurry, bright yellow smiley face peering closely at Dev. He propped himself upright and looked around the familiar medical bay in the Inventory. His "uncle", Charles Parker, was standing at the end of his bed with his arms folded. He pushed his glasses further up the bridge of his nose as he studied Dev.

"How are you feeling, Devon?" he asked, with little discernible concern in his voice.

Dev swung his feet off the end of the bed and stretched. He was wearing a pair of shorts and could see his bare arms and legs clearly. His heart skipped a beat: there wasn't a scratch on them.

"As good as new," he said after a moment. He caught a thin smile crossing his uncle's lips. Then he suddenly remembered what had happened. "The Collector! He was there!"

"Yes. The others gave a report. Well, what I could make of it; Mason's spelling is atrocious. Eema had to translate it. So, he was after the SonicBoom."

Dev stood up and stretched, and every joint in his body seemed to crack. "It didn't seem like much of an artefact to bring the Collector out of. . ." He was about to say retirement, but they had all assumed the villain was dead.

"Never underestimate the small," Charles said. "Well, Mason, Riya and Aaron came to your rescue."

Dev looked expectantly at him, waiting for more.

The silence lasted an overly long time.

"How?" Dev finally asked, with an impatient sigh.

His uncle pursed his lips before continuing. "Oh, the usual. Lots of shouting, some destruction. Bringing the Avrocar in so Joe Public got to see it all. The Collector slipped away with Winter Storm empty-handed."

"Winter Storm – is that what that robot thing was?"

"Yes. The Moroccan government were very understanding, but perhaps next time you could do things a little more low-key. We never want a repeat of Hong Kong. Or Tokyo. Or—"

"I get the message."

"Well, you're on your feet. Good." He clapped his hands together, then rubbed them, trying to think of something else to say.

After another uncomfortable pause, Dev spoke up. "So, that's it? He gets away. I'm fixed up . . . and nobody is going to ask any questions?"

"Such as?"

"Why the Collector wants the SonicBoom? Why he's suddenly turned up? And what exactly is Winter Storm, and how do we stop it next time?" Another question was burning on Dev's lips, but he kept that to himself.

Charles gave a little chuckle. "Ah, the bio-bot. Now that is exactly why we need you back on your feet."

Dev shifted uncomfortably in his seat as Eema projected a holographic display into the middle of the canteen where the tables had been cleared away. The Scavengers were sitting in a random assortment of chairs, with Sergeant Wade and Tyker standing off to the side.

The Inventory was run by the World Consortium, a secret international government branch. But for such a rich organization, Dev marvelled that they couldn't even provide a basic briefing room. Instead the large canteen looked bland, with its squeaky-clean white plastic walls and the newly installed speaker system that constantly played international music. No, *muzak*, as a technician had told them. Music designed to be so bland it made people want to leave and go back to work.

Dev kept getting distracted by the sidelong glances Lot was throwing him from a few feet away, further along the table. They hadn't spoken since he'd woken up, and he was desperate for details from Marrakech. He forced his attention back to a three-dimensional depiction of Winter Storm revolving over the floor.

"Winter Storm sounds cool," stated Aaron, tapping his palm against a table for emphasis. "Onslow Winter is a genius!"

Onslow Winter had been a role model for Aaron all his life, he'd revealed. Growing up, he had bought all Winter's latest tech and had taught himself computer coding so he could be just like his hero one day.

"And instead you became a hacker with those skills,"

said Riya, rolling her eyes. "Isn't that how you got recruited for this?"

"Oh, yeah..." Aaron said, grinning widely.

"Well, Winter Storm may be cool," cautioned Sergeant Wade, "but as with all new technology, if it's in the wrong hands, bad things usually happen."

"And the right hands are our hands," said Riya, with a trace of sarcasm that went over Wade's head.

"Exactly! Now Onslow is aware of World Consortium's existence." Wade sounded particularly stressed, as she had recently been placed in control of the whole organization. "Fortunately, he is cooperating with us to discover if he has a leak inside his company –"

Aaron sprang from his seat with excitement. "We're working with Onslow Winter?"

Mason sniggered under his breath. "Nerd..."

"Winter made his fortune by designing those brilliant mobile phones. He put half of Africa on the internet for free too!"

"I thought he was already dead," said Riya. "Isn't he, like, fifty or something? He's ancient."

"No," Aaron snapped back defensively. "He was very ill. Something everybody said he wouldn't recover from. But he did. Because he's that awesome!"

Wade gestured for Aaron to sit back down. "Winter Tech is almost as secure as we are, so how the Collector knew about the bio-bots before the launch is a puzzle. If there is a mole in the company, then it may be a way to track the Collector down."

Aaron's mouth hung open in amazement. "Wow! I'm going to actually meet him!"

The others spluttered with laughter at his hero worship.

Aaron tilted his head and gasped at the ceiling in exasperation. "You don't get it, do you? We just store the stuff here, like a museum. Winter? He's the guy actually making the stuff that ends up here. Can you imagine what they're developing that we don't know about? Without him or inventors like him, we'd just be—"

"Normal," Dev blurted out. He had no idea why. Before the Inventory had been raided, he had often thought about who his parents were and had longed for a normal family. His uncle had always been vague about their fate, until Dev discovered that he'd never had a family. If it weren't for the technology in the Inventory, he wouldn't have existed at all.

Wade smiled at Aaron. "That's right. Winter may be brilliant, but he's just another guy who puts his pants on one leg at a time."

"I bet he does both at the same time!"

Wade ignored him. "Your mission is to go to Winter Tech and work out if there is a leak."

"That sounds boooorrrrring," said Riya, slumping in her chair.

Mason spoke up, surprised to find himself siding with Aaron. "Are you kidding? We get to be detectives!"

Lot leaned over towards Dev and whispered, "How are you feeling?"

"Completely fine." He tried to focus on whatever Wade was saying, but his attention was distracted again when she gently squeezed his hand.

"You were in bad shape in Morocco. Did they just stitch you together, or..." Dev knew she wanted to say *is it a new you*, but they had yet to tell the others about their discovery in the Black Zone. And Dev was happy to keep it that way.

"I'm the same old me," he whispered back, a little too defensively. The thought of his mind being sucked from his dead body and being downloaded into a new one disturbed him. So he clung to the belief that it hadn't happened, that the clones they had discovered were just unused backups for a sick experiment his uncle had yet to perform.

But the truth was, he couldn't be sure.

A groan from the others got their attention. Tyker was shrugging while everybody else was rolling their eyes at something.

"I take it you're fine with that, Dev?" Wade asked him.

Dev nodded. "Of course I am," he said, forcing a smile and wondering just what he had agreed to.

Aaron was giddy from the second they left to the moment they pulled up at Winter House in a black minibus with tinted windows. Onslow Winter's HQ was perched on a mountainside, accessible only by a single snaking road, and offered incredible views of the local fishing town far below. They were in California, far north of San Francisco, just south of the Oregon border. The air was sharp and fresh, with a light autumnal fog clinging to the forested landscape.

Aaron became excited again as the building came into view. It looked like an enormous golf ball had landed on the mountain. Standing thirty storeys tall, it was packed with research labs for all Winter's technological innovations. Aaron had incessantly talked about how eco-friendly the solar-powered geodesic design was;

about the ultra-reinforced graphene superstructure that made it the toughest building in the world; the revolutionary earthquake stabilization rig that would keep it perfectly level even in the fiercest Californian quake. Nobody interrupted him; they were all just hoping he'd run out of things to say ... but he didn't.

Tyker led the team inside, much to Dev's annoyance.

"Why do we suddenly need him babysitting?" he muttered to Mason as they entered a massive, brightly lit atrium. The white stone walls and zinc panels reflected sunlight from every angle, forcing Dev to squint as his eyes adjusted.

"That's what I said," said Mason. "So why did you agree when Wade mentioned it before we left?"

They were greeted by an assistant dressed in the black jeans and polo-necked shirt that seemed to be the company uniform. He led them to Winter's office at the top of the building, which offered a 360-degree view of the forest around them.

Before Tyker could introduce himself, Aaron pushed forward and shook the hand of a startled Onslow Winter.

"Mr Winter, I think you're incredible!" he blurted.

Riya and Lot shook their heads. "So uncool," said

Riya sadly, sighing and chewing away at a piece of gum.

Mason stood next to Riya and casually put his hands in his pockets. "I know, right. Sad. Totally . . . not sick."

Lot barely suppressed a giggle. "He looks older in real life, doesn't he?" she whispered.

Winter finally extracted his hand from Aaron's grip and regarded the team. "Well, you guys are not quite what I was expecting! But your Sergeant Wade did warn me you were something special. I don't take people at face value, so if you can do the things she says you can, that's good enough for me."

Tyker stepped between Aaron and Winter, subtly nudging Aaron back. "We had the briefing about Winter Storm. Living machines – that's a remarkable achievement."

"And one that wasn't known beyond these walls." Winter gestured around the room, then paced to the nearest window. "We even grew the bio-bots here."

"Grew?" said Dev. "You mean 'made'?"

Winter gave a wry smile. "That's the beauty of biotechnology: it's alive. Like a plant or an insect. Alive. Capable of motion. And with many of them together, capable of problem solving."

"But a plant can't solve problems, and we saw that thing adjust its strategy after we blasted it apart," said Lot.

Winter turned and looked at her. "Really? Plants evolve through time to tackle environmental problems around them. They create ingenious ways of ensuring their seeds spread. They move to track the sun, and even communicate by releasing chemicals. And insects – look at ants and bees. On their own you would think they're dumb bugs, but collectively they share what we call a hive mind. Thousands of individuals capable of cooperating to solve bigger problems for the benefit of the whole."

He was warming to his topic, and sat on the edge of his desk. "There is a limit to traditional electronics known as Moore's law."

"I know this!" Aaron said, bouncing from foot to foot like the keenest kid in class. "The number of transistors in a chip doubles every two years to increase processing speed."

"Exactly," said Winter with a smile. "The problem is, eventually we run out of space within a microchip. Make them bigger, that means the electrons have to travel further, which slows it all down." He held up his little finger. "Now, imagine a small, basic living brain, like that of an ant. Already it is capable of more processing power than a normal silicon chip you'd find in your phone."

"Not my phone," Riya muttered under her breath.

She held her prized device tightly in her hand: it was a phone from the Inventory, packed with technology that would likely surprise the genius in front of her.

Winter drew his other little finger to the first. "Add another brain that can share the workload of the first and we suddenly have even more processing power." He waggled all his fingers. "And more and more . . . and we now have a living bio-computer capable of far more than any regular computer out there."

"Like the processor in Eema," Dev said aloud. Eema ran on a biochip that had been seized by the World Consortium and modified for her, upgrading her more traditional computer brain and bringing the Inventory's artificially intelligent computer system to life. And being a living chip, it was one of the things out of reach of Dev's synaesthesia.

"Exactly," Winter said.

It took a moment for Dev to be surprised by Winter's response. Winter had only just been told about the Consortium; surely he didn't know about the secrets inside the Inventory!

Onslow Winter chuckled knowingly. "I created that chip, and your Consortium stole it from me. They thought it was too powerful for the world to have." He shot a scathing look at Tyker. "But they still used it for their own purposes. They even asked me to consult on the design. That theft put my work back by half a decade. It is the reason I keep the strictest security here."

"Yet somebody in your company is a spy for the Collector," said Dev. "And we need to know who."

"People always leave a trail," said Riya.

Winter shrugged. "We do the most comprehensive background checks on all our staff. Our computer system is one of the most secure in the world. My security team have found nothing suspicious."

Dev sat behind Winter's desk and drew the computer keyboard nearer. He cracked his knuckles, then placed his fingers on the keyboard.

"Good luck with that," said Winter sarcastically. "We have password encryption that governments can only dream about—"

"I'm in," said Dev, trying not to smile too smugly at the expression of utter disbelief on Winter's face. "And I've identified some unusual communications from one member of your team."

Winter finally found his voice. "Who?"

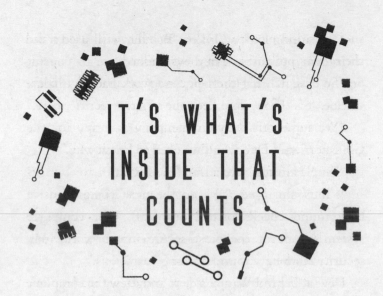

IT'S WHAT'S INSIDE THAT COUNTS

A heavy hand thumped the vending machine hard, but still the packet of choco drops refused to budge from the very tip of the corkscrew mechanism holding them. They bobbed tantalizingly over the drop.

"Oh, crud!" said Security Chief Dolton Hammer. "A billion dollars of technology in this place and they still don't have a vending machine that works!"

He gripped the side of the machine, intending to rock it – but stopped when he realized his boss was standing behind him. "Oh, Mr Winter, sir. Just dealing with a, um, technical issue."

Dev stood next to Onslow Winter, with Tyker and the others further back in the corridor.

"So I see, Chief Hammer. And your solution is brute force."

"Whatever gets the job done, sir."

"My friends here would like a word with you."

Chief Hammer smiled. He was a tall man, but his huge muscular bulk made him almost half as wide at the shoulders. He bent over to address Dev as adults do when they have never been around young people. "Sure. What can I help you with, sonny?"

"We'd like you to try a new gadget we made at the science fair," said Dev in an over-the-top yokel farmer accent. Hammer didn't think anything of it, but Lot chuckled quietly.

Dev waved her over. She held up what looked like a large watch.

"Ah, some new wearable tech?" Hammer asked, taking the watch and clamping it to his wrist. "I got one of those fitness step counter things at home. Waste of time."

Lot flashed an innocent smile. "Sort of the same, except this one checks over one hundred physical and psychological signs to see if you're lying. I call it the Lie-Pod."

Hammer's face darkened as he looked at Winter. His hand immediately went to remove the device, but the clasp, which had been so simple to attach, had now seamlessly vanished into a solid ring around his wrist.

"I'm not doing this!" he cried.

Winter shrugged. "What's the problem? Surely you have nothing to hide? You are my head of security, after all."

"It won't hurt," said Dev. "Much. . ."

Winter looked his chief squarely in the eye. "I just want to know why a petabyte of data was sent from your computer to an untraceable address several days before we launched Winter Storm."

"I don't know what you're talking about!" snarled Hammer. "This is an outrage – OW!" His hand went for the device on his wrist as pain shot up his arm. The Lie-Pod refused to budge.

"Sorry about that," said Dev in a voice that clearly said he wasn't. "It's firing a pulse through your nervous system to measure how truthful that statement was."

"I didn't send anything! ARGH!" he howled again, rubbing his forearm.

Dev shrugged apologetically. "The Lie-Pod wasn't entirely finished, so it has a few painful little quirks. Especially when it detects a lie."

"I'm ... not ... lying!" growled Hammer through gritted teeth as he dropped to his knees, clutching his wrist, which was turning purple.

"Maybe we should remove it," said Lot with concern. "You never know; like most of the stuff we get, it might be faulty."

Onslow Winter wasn't listening. His face was twisted in rage as he stood over his security chief. "YOU LIE!" he bellowed.

"I should just check that—" Dev started to say as he knelt at Hammer's side and touched the Lie-Pod.

"NO!" Hammer lashed out with a muscular arm the size of a tree branch and batted Dev so hard into the vending machine that the glass cracked and his choco drops fell. The security chief pulled a shock baton from his belt and thumbed the power button. Sparks crackled across the tip.

Lot was the first to react. She let fly a *chapa baixa* kick, a capoeira dance-fighting technique that Riya had been teaching her. It struck Hammer across his thigh, dropping him back to his knees as he tried to stand and causing him to drop the shock baton. But before Lot could land properly, Hammer snapped out and grabbed her foot in mid-air. With a twist, he sent Lot corkscrewing through the air and into the wall.

"LOT!" Her name tumbled from Dev's lips as he felt anger course through him. Without any conscious decision, his synaesthesia surged through his entire body, crackling into every bit of the vending machine he was crumpled against.

With a flash of sparks from the shelves around him, the corkscrew mechanisms screamed as their motors turned at high speed – propelling chocolate bars and packets of crisps outward. As Hammer climbed to his feet the remaining glass around him broke, pelting him with confectionery. He held his arm across his face as the snacks struck him with the force of rubber bullets before they burst from impact.

He staggered against the corridor wall as crisps rained down around him like salty snowflakes. Dev may have been surprised by his own instinctive use of his power, but that was nothing on how surprised he was to see Hammer suddenly convulse as *something* rippled under his skin.

As Aaron rushed to check Winter was OK, Mason couldn't tear his gaze from Hammer writhing on the floor.

"That's either the world's worst breakdancing or something real bad is happening."

The security chief's body was undulating under his uniform as if ferrets had been let loose. Then his shrieks became shrill as the cloth around his shoulders tore open and streamers of smoke broke out.

Dev blinked in surprise. It wasn't smoke. It was a stream of bio-bot particles that oozed from his pores and formed into long tentacles. Another two pairs erupted from the back of his thighs, then his spine. Two whipped through the air and wrapped around Dev, hoisting him off the ground and crushing the breath from him.

The second pair lashed at Onslow Winter and Aaron.

Aaron was stupefied as Winter pushed him in front of himself, as a shield. Aaron had just enough presence of mind to throw himself flat as the unfolding bio-tentacles snapped over his head.

Winter slapped the buckle on his belt. A shield of amber suddenly blossomed from the buckle, encompassing him completely, like a statue. The tentacles bounced harmlessly from the armour and he toppled over on to the floor, frozen in position.

The last set of tentacles reached for Mason and Riya. Riya jumped, her body twisting in an elegant capoeira move. Hammer's extra limb ripped into the plaster wall where her head had been.

Mason wasn't so lucky and the limb wrapped around him, hoisting him off his feet. He gasped as the coils tightened. "Dev . . . do something!"

Trying to ignore the pain, Dev focused his synaesthesia, forcing it to explore the tendril squeezing him. But nothing happened; he had no synaesthetic reaction to it. He tried to warn the others, but he hadn't the breath left. The room started to spin and his vision blurred.

Tyker threw himself flat along the floor. Hammer's limbs struck down at the ground to skewer him – but he slid past the first and rolled aside from a second as he reached Hammer's dropped shock baton. He was almost at the feet of the big man as three more whirling tentacles lashed out above Hammer's head.

Before they could stab him, Tyker thrust the baton into Hammer's thigh and discharged a high-voltage shock. Hammer roared in pain and stumbled backwards, his new artificial limbs thrashing wildly. Dev and Mason were released from their choking grip as Hammer writhed in agony, the bio-bot limbs vibrating in a blur like a dying fly thrashing its wings.

Dev stood first, helping Aaron pull Lot to her feet.

"Can you walk?" he asked urgently.

Lot nodded, her eyes on Hammer as he quickly recovered from the shock and regained control of his limbs. "Better yet, I can run!"

"Run!" Dev yelled to the others.

"We've got to stop him!" said Aaron, looking between Dev and Hammer.

"My synaesthesia doesn't work on him. I've got nothing else!" Dev cried. Sergeant Wade hadn't armed them with anything useful, not expecting this assignment to develop into a full-fledged fight so quickly.

Mason crawled on all fours as Hammer regained the use of one tentacle and slammed it down, just missing him. Mason sprang to his feet and pushed Aaron towards the door. "Stop standing around!"

Aaron hesitated as he reached Onslow Winter, who was encased in his amber shell. He could just see the man inside unmoving, unblinking. "What about Winter?"

"He'll be protected in that," said Tyker, now pushing Aaron as he caught up with him.

Dev and Lot reached the door first, Dev holding it open as the others rushed through. Riya brought up the rear and glanced behind her in time to see Hammer clamber to his feet. The six tentacles hoisted his body into the air, so he lay almost horizontal, carried forward like some giant insect.

Riya swapped a horrified look with Dev, before they both heaved the door shut. Seconds later it shook from repeated hits from behind. Dev slapped the control panel, his gift communicating with the system and ordering the door to lock. Then they followed the others through the maze of corridors.

"Is it this way?" asked Mason as they reached a junction. Every branching corridor looked the same. Winter had led them at speed down several storeys into the security levels, talking the whole way, so nobody had paid any attention to the route they'd taken.

Riya shivered at the memory of grotesque man-thing. "What happened to him?"

"They were inside him," said Lot, recalling how the man had changed before their eyes. "They were the same as the bio-bots in Marrakech, right?"

Tyker nodded. "I think so."

"If they're sort of alive, does that mean they can infect people?"

"Like a cold virus?" said Aaron thoughtfully.

Lot nodded. "Yeah. But not quite as small, I suppose."

Tyker wagged a finger. "Now you see the need for places like the Inventory. Even the most well-intentioned invention can have side effects and unintended consequences."

"I couldn't sense the bio-bots," said Dev, looking at his hands. "If they're living creatures, then ... there's nothing I can do." The disturbing prospect that the bio-bots could infect a human host was overshadowed by the sudden thought he and his powers may be redundant.

"That's disgusting," said Aaron, shivering. "Could they get into us? Do ... *that to us!*"

They all exchanged worried looks.

Riya shivered again and scratched her arm, imagining she felt a bio-bot crawling across it. "You saw his face. It was as if he didn't know..."

Just then a loud crash behind them made them all turn. Seconds later, the reinforced security door was tossed around the corner. It was twisted and buckled, like a crushed tin can.

Then Chief Hammer turned the corner, suspended from ceiling by his six new limbs, like a grotesque insect. Another mass of bio-bots had grown over his eyes into a single antenna which swung towards them.

"I see you!" he growled in a voice that was barely his. Then the monstrosity charged towards them.

SHAKE IT OFF

A frightened scream from his left almost deafened Dev. It was Aaron, who stood with an outstretched, trembling finger pointing at the hybrid Chief Hammer as he scurried towards them.

Lot shot out a hand to cover Aaron's mouth. "Shut up!"

At the same time, Dev reached out for the nearest fire alarm. His power spread through the system, activating it. He had expected the sprinkler system to unleash water, but instead a spray of gas shot from the fire suppression system in the ceiling; the delicate technology within the building was too fragile for water.

But the thick smoke had the desired effect. Red

emergency lights flashed all across the building as the fire alarm sounded. On the floors above them, the staff at Winter Tech began an orderly evacuation, oblivious to the deadly fight in the bowels of the building.

The gas obscured their view of Hammer, but it had an unexpected effect: as soon as the gas touched the metal corridor, it made the surface slippery – so slick that Hammer's bio-limbs lost their grip on the ceiling and he thudded to the ground.

"This way!" said Tyker, already running down one of the branching corridors.

They took the next right, then the next left, moving in a zigzag away from their pursuer. The corridor around them turned from a tidy white wall to more industrial grey. Pipes and electrical cables now ran along the walls and ceiling as they entered the grimy service areas of Winter Tech.

"We didn't come this way," said Mason, looking around with mounting panic. "Have you got us lost?"

Tyker stopped at the next junction and held up a finger to silence them. He strained to listen for sounds of pursuit behind them. All they could hear was the gas hissing from the sprinklers overhead, creating a veil of fog. Then he spoke in a whisper.

"If we're lost ... then we may have also lost him."

Another moment of silence ... before Lot slapped Tyker on the shoulder. "That's the most stupid escape plan I have ever heard!"

Before Tyker could defend himself, they all spun around. There was the unmistakable sound of rapid scuttling, like a giant insect moving down the passage behind.

"There!" The words barely came from Riya's lips as she pointed at a stairwell several metres away.

Light on their feet, they hurried down the metal steps, entering a massive basement of thick pipes and humming machinery. They had entered the bowels of the Winter House. Through the jets of gas, they could just see huge hydraulic rams three storeys high, anchored to the ceiling and stretching into the floor.

Aaron looked around in awe. "Wow! This is the earthquake stabilization rig I told you about!"

"The what?" said Mason, confused. Like the others, he hadn't listened to a word of Aaron's tour-guide lecture.

"I think you've led us into a dead end," Dev said to Tyker.

The stairwell they had descended suddenly shuddered as the Hammer-Thing put its weight on it.

Everybody fled for cover. Dev crouched next to a massive cylinder that had thick rubber cables running from it, connecting to one of the rams. He just caught sight of Riya and Mason squeezing into a dark space between machinery before he lost sight of them behind a plume of gas.

He held his breath as the metal grating on the floor quivered, indicating Hammer had descended. Dev strained to listen; against the thrum of machinery, it was difficult to pick out any new sounds.

Sure enough, the gentle clatter of six limbs slowly walking could *just* be heard.

The steps were getting louder. Closer.

Dev attempted to push himself further into the recess, but there was only a solid slab of metal behind him as Hammer drew closer. From his new position, Dev could now see across the corridor, where Lot was crouching in the shadows. Like him, she was trapped between machinery, but unfortunately her cover was ruined by a red, strobing emergency light that revealed her position in the darkness with every flicker.

Metal tapping echoed from the mist. It sounded much closer than before. He tried to get Lot's attention with a wave, but she couldn't see him. Then she twitched, her hand rapidly rubbing her nose in the unmistakable gesture that indicated she was trying everything she could not to sneeze.

That would be a death sentence.

Dev laid his hand across the metal behind him and probed it with his synaesthesia, praying he could make a connection. But with no electronics to hook on to, his power was useless.

Then Dev's blood ran cold as a black snake slithered across the floor. It took him a moment to realize that it was the single extended eye that had sprouted from Hammer's forehead. This close he could see the smooth bio-bot surface ripple and pulse as if breathing. The tip was a black orb, reminding him of a snail's eye as it swept side to side.

Time seemed to slow as the eye swivelled towards him. With no gadgets, no usable power, Dev was a sitting duck. In all his adventures he had put his faith in technology. Now he was facing certain death. And he knew once Hammer had got him, Lot would be next.

With that revelation, an icy calm gripped Dev. No, he wouldn't go down without a fight.

He would go down swinging.

At that very moment, Lot sneezed, and the eye

jerked around as Lot was bathed in the red emergency illumination. With a clatter, the Hammer-Thing ran into view, blocking Dev's only exit from his hiding place.

As the hybrid scuttered closely past, he could see Hammer's human body was little more than a limp form carried by the insectile legs. A fine network of black veins criss-crossed his skin, and his uniform was torn from where lines of bio-bots reached out like weeds across the man. Dev doubted that Chief Hammer had volunteered to host such an infection, but that raised more questions that he didn't have time to think about.

With a scream of frustration, Dev rushed from his hiding place and used both hands to rip the thick rubber pipe from the side of the hydraulic ram. He thrust it into the Hammer-Thing's side as high-pressure, heated oil shot out at great force. The creature howled as the jet punched into him, spraying bio-bots in every direction, sending him tumbling down the metal corridor.

Lot pulled herself out of the recess and joined Dev. They watched Hammer writhing on the floor as the bio-bots dispersed, sluiced away by the oil and disappearing down grates in the floor. Tyker, Riya, Mason and Aaron slowly emerged from their hiding places to watch.

"Quick thinking," Mason said with an appreciative nod.

Tyker edged forward and carefully extended his leg to nudge Hammer's foot.

The security chief twitched.

Tyker looked up at the others. "That was easy. Now the question is. . ."

Aaron suddenly pulled Tyker away from Hammer. "Get back!"

The hydraulic fluid looked as if it was oozing in reverse, back up through the grating and dripping down from the walls and ceiling where it had splattered. The bio-bots were re-forming into their host.

"This is so not good!" Riya said, backing up.

"Did Winter give any indication of how we kill these bots?" asked Mason.

Tyker shook his head. "I think it's time to run again."

"And how long are we going to run for?" said Dev, memories of the streets of Marrakech still fresh in his mind. "We've got to stop this thing now."

"I have zero suggestions," said Aaron, backing away.

Dev looked around for anything that could help them. He saw a series of cables sparking as they dangled from the hydraulic ram he had damaged.

"Hold on tight," said Dev as he rushed for them.

"What is that supposed to mean?" Tyker asked, his eyes firmly on Hammer as the bio-bots swarmed over his body, slowly lifting it from the floor.

Lot clasped her arms around a nearby metal pole. "When Dev says things like that, I've learned not to ask. Just do."

Dev clutched the wires in his hand, flinching as a spark nipped his skin. He focused his synaesthesia through the system, tapping into the building's control system. It was now a simple matter of *willing* the earthquake rams to extend.

The bio-tentacles began to extend from Hammer once again, slowly growing as the bots continued to reassemble from around the room.

Mason reached out to nudge Dev. "Whatever you're doing, do it faster!"

The entire room suddenly trembled as Dev took control of the enormous rams. Designed to move centimetres at a time to counter an earthquake, he was not sure how they would respond when instructed to fully extend at speed.

With a boom, every ram along one side extended a dozen metres in the same direction. There was no time for any pre-warning — the room tilted forty-five degrees.

The only one not to have heeded Dev's warning, Riya was thrown off her feet and began to slide towards Hammer. The Hammer-Thing was catapulted backwards through the air — its six still-forming tentacles flailing out and snagging machinery around it to stop its fall. It hung, suspended like an insect in a web, its tentacles spread in every direction.

Riya rolled on to her front, her fingers scraping across the metal grating as she tried to stop herself from skidding into the monster. But it was impossible. Two of Hammer's limbs released their hold and stretched for her.

With one arm and leg, Dev held on to a steel pipe. His free hand held the cables tightly. He immediately reversed one set of rams, lowering the building — and at the same time extended the opposite set.

The room around them seesawed in the opposite direction. Riya slid to a halt. She caught her breath ... then screamed as she began to slide back the way she'd come, just out of reach of the groping tentacles. The Hammer-Thing released its grip and tumbled after her.

The building's earthquake system was not designed for such massive changes in direction. From the car park, the evacuated staff watched in astonishment as the hydraulic rams severed from their anchor points on the mountain. Electrical cables and pipes sheered away as the entire building was torn from the ground.

With a mighty rumble, it rolled down the side of the mountain. The geodesic graphene structure absorbed every impact, preventing the building from tearing apart. Like a wrecking ball, the enormous building crashed into the forest, tearing a massive trench through the landscape.

Inside, it was as if they were trapped in a washing machine spinning at high speed. They clung on, arms going numb from the effort. It felt as if gravity was increasing as they were pulled in rapidly changing directions. The Hammer-Thing was about to grasp Riya when it was hurled at speed into a wall – then into the ceiling, then another wall. It pinballed rapidly from view.

Riya would have done the same, except Tyker reached out for her and, using all his strength, held on tight.

After several bounds, the building rolled from a cliff – slamming down through the town below. People fled in panic, vehicles swerving aside as Winter House gained momentum and thundered over shops and houses like a bowling ball over matchboxes. Cars were crushed, radio masts and electrical pylons smashed apart as Winter Tech bounded for the harbour.

The building was unstoppable as it shot from the side of the quay – destroying a dozen fishing boats as it skimmed across the ocean's surface. A huge wave broke before it, rapidly slowing the rotation. For a moment, the building bobbed in the water – before rapidly sinking in a torrent of white water. It came to a stop on its side as it hit the seabed, three-quarters submerged.

Crowds of spectators gathered on the quay to watch, while others pushed out small rowing boats to check for survivors.

After escaping by swimming through a broken window, Aaron broke the surface first, his arm around Mason, who was floundering and gasping for breath as he spluttered, "I'm rubbish at swimming!"

"Stop thrashing around or you'll drown us both," Aaron growled.

Lot and Dev broke the surface next, gasping for breath, as their lungs were about to burst. They trod water and looked around...

"Riya?" Lot said, spitting out water as a wave struck her in the face.

Everybody twisted to see. Between the waves and a growing layer of debris from the building's offices, they couldn't see anybody else. The thought of their friend being trapped inside made them all feel sick...

Then Riya broke free with a gasp as she scrambled on to a floating desk. She fought for breath, clinging to the wood with all her might. Dev swam over to her, pushing the increasing amount of floating junk aside.

"Riya? Are you OK?"

She managed a nod.

"Where's Tyker?"

Riya closed her eyes and wordlessly shook her head.

The shock Dev felt was like a physical blow to the chest. They had lost a member of the team.

'CISCO

Sitting on the tailgates of ambulances, sipping warm cocoa and shivering under silver thermal blankets, Dev and the others waited for Sergeant Wade and a platoon of Consortium troops to turn up to handle the disaster scene.

They had kept away from the increasing number of reporters who showed up, chasing the story of how Onslow Winter's building had rolled into the sea. Onslow himself had been retrieved from the submerged wreckage by Consortium salvage troops. He was still encased in amber, in a state of suspended animation and unable to move, but still alive. Just. He had been airlifted back to the Inventory to be chipped out. They had also found Tyker's body.

Riya recounted how he had held on to her as the building began to roll about them. He'd managed to haul her into a nook, in which she could brace herself with her hands and feet. While doing so, he hadn't see a bio-tentacle lash around his neck and snatch him into the rolling room.

Riya sat quietly, staring at her feet. So far, the divers hadn't found any sign of Hammer or the bio-bots, but it was thought the search could take a whole week due to salvage difficulties and an approaching storm front.

Mason pointed to the Osprey aircraft, a military VTOL – which stood for Vertical Takeoff and Landing – that sat in a car park with its two helicopter blades still thundering as the covered stretcher carrying Tyker was pushed up the ramp. "Aren't we going back with . . . him?" He couldn't bring himself to say Tyker's name. As if saying it would make the situation more real.

Wade shook her head. "No. You're still on mission." She stepped away to take a call, and the team silently watched the Osprey take off vertically, its wing-mounted propellers pivoting to become horizontal, transforming into a regular aircraft as it zoomed over the bay.

Wade returned, hanging up her phone. "Winter had provided details of his bio-bots that our engineers are still working on. Norman seems to think that an unintended use of the bots is their ability to infect other people. Like you saw with the security chief."

"Like a virus," said Aaron, as it confirmed his suspicions.

"Similar, yes. As you know, the bot team used insects, primarily ants, as their basis for developing a hive mind. It seems they actually cloned insect brains and nervous structures. Our current understanding is that insects can learn, but not think. Winter's creations could do both, which meant for safety they introduced another element as a controller. In the jungle, there is a type of fungus that preys on ants – all types of insects, in fact."

"A fungus, like a mushroom that hunts ants?" Mason said with scepticism.

"*Ophiocordyceps unilateralis,*" Wade said icily. Dev frowned. She was acting very irritable with them.

Wade continued, wafting a hand dismissively in Mason's direction. "It grows into ants' brains and controls them. Winter's bio-bots are a little more sophisticated than that, but they seem to have the same party trick. We need to talk to Winter to know more."

"Huh, then chip the coward out of his little amber box," said Aaron bitterly. His adoration of Onslow Winter had vaporized the moment his hero had tried to use him as a human shield.

Wade continued. "So there's a possibility that the bots can receive outside signals or instructions."

"You think that security guard was being controlled?" asked Lot.

Wade nodded. "Undoubtedly. Think about that for a moment. What if a crowd was infected? Or a world leader? All without their knowledge? What if they could be instructed to do *anything* you wanted?"

She let the implications of that seep in.

"You're saying Chief Hammer was innocent?" Dev finally said. "That he didn't kill Tyker?"

Sergeant Wade sucked in a long breath. "Not consciously. I think that's a possibility."

"Even if Hammer was controlled, who inside Winter's company knew about the bio-bots and infected him?"

"We need to find that out. And quickly. Which is why you five are still on mission. If there are more infected people out there, we need to know about it. And you can start by visiting the location Chief

Hammer sent huge amounts of data to. Eema will send you the details."

Dev glanced up at the Osprey, which was now just a dark smudge in the sky. "And what about Tyker?"

Wade turned and looked at Dev with a piercing stare. Her face was pale, and he noticed dark rings under her eyes from lack of sleep. Or had she been crying?

"He's dead, Devon. Nobody comes back from that."

The mood in the car was tense for a number of reasons. Sergeant Wade had given them a satchel of gadgets so they didn't once again find themselves completely defenceless, and had put the team, weighed down heavily with Tyker's death, into a car to be sent into San Francisco.

After a minute or two, Mason turned around from the driver's seat. "Does anybody want to swap places? This is freaking me out." He gestured to the steering wheel as the car accelerated to fifty miles per hour along the winding Pacific Coast Highway.

"Relax," said Aaron. "It's the latest driverless tech out of Silicon Valley. It's supposed to be safer than a real driver."

Mason watched as the wheel turned by itself as they

took a bend in the road. He glanced at the flimsy road barrier to his side and the rocky drop to the crashing ocean waves below. He pulled a face.

"I don't know about you lot, but I'm really starting to mistrust technology." When nobody volunteered to swap seats, Mason returned to rummaging through the gadget satchel to see what they had been given. But his mind wasn't on it and he dropped the bag on the floor. "And I don't think it's right that the only one who knows exactly where we're going – is the car!"

Wade had told them some vague details. Eema had traced the data dump from Winter Tech to a computer in downtown San Francisco. She hoped there they would find a lead on the Collector's whereabouts.

The vehicle was electric, so the only sound came from the soft, monotonous drone of the tyres against asphalt. Mason couldn't settle in the silence, so he turned around in his seat again. "And why is it she couldn't have brought in the Avro so we could have flown in? It would have been quicker."

Riya sighed. "Mase?"

He looked at her expectantly.

"Shut up."

With a huff, Mason turned back in his seat and

folded his arms tighter. Then his hand went for the car's radio – or where it should have been. Instead there was just a blank panel. Evidently, the designer had thought a driverless car wouldn't want to listen to the radio on a long trip.

After three hours, the rolling, vine-clad hills gave way and the orange pinnacles of the Golden Gate Bridge came into view. Lot leaned forward for a better look and was disappointed that fog was already rolling into the bay. By the time they were crossing the iconic bridge, the fog had thickened so they couldn't even see to the top of the suspension cables.

The streets of San Francisco undulated with steep hills that on first glance looked almost impossible to drive up. Their car diligently stopped as cable trams rattled past with scores of tourists and commuters clinging on, disappearing into the thickening mist.

The car eventually pulled up outside a row of three-storey houses in the Pacific Heights neighbourhood. Each home was structurally identical but painted in a range of lively colours, built on a sharply sloping hill. Despite the incline, the car effortlessly parked in an empty space. It took a moment for them to realize the electric engine had shut off.

Lot opened the rear door and climbed out, regarding the house. "This is the one. Well, I suppose we can just go up and knock."

Aaron followed her. "That's a dumb idea."

Riya, Mason and Dev stepped out from the other side of the vehicle.

"Let's hear *your* brilliant idea, then," said Lot.

Aaron looked away. He didn't have one.

"Good. Let's get this over with." She trotted up the stone steps leading to the front door and stabbed the doorbell twice before anybody could stop her. The others hung back, but Dev joined her just as the door partially opened and a bald man poked his head around.

"What?" he said in a gruff tone.

Lot's face lit up in a broad, innocent smile. "Hi! We just moved in down the street —" she waved a hand vaguely in that direction "— and our internet connection just went down. Couple of other people have complained too, so I wondered if you had—"

"It's fine," the man snapped, his eyes darting up and down the street before falling on the others standing around the car. He began to push the door closed.

Dev looked desperately at Lot. Whatever she had

thought her plan would reveal, it was clearly not working. He suddenly spoke up.

"Can we see?" He cringed inside as he realized just how awkward that sounded. "We need to message the broadband company..."

The bald man stopped pushing the door and studied Dev. For a few seconds, Dev thought his clumsy tactic was going to work ... but the man's expression slowly turned to one of recognition.

"Wait ... I know you." He looked from Dev to Lot. "You're—" With a startled yelp, he slammed the door in their faces.

Lot shook her head and patted Dev on the shoulder. "He's confusing you with somebody famous."

"Unless he's been warned who to look out for," said Dev under his breath, glancing around, hoping for inspiration to strike. "What do we do?"

The answer came seconds later when the door was blown off its hinges.

Lot had started walking back down towards the car, and as a result, Dev got the full force of the door against his shoulder and side. As he fell, he knocked into Lot, who rolled down the steps ahead of him. Dev slid down two steps before the weight of the door increased painfully on his back, pinning him down, as the bald man accelerated from the house on a motocross bike.

The bike soared off the front door steps – forcing Riya, Aaron and Mason to duck – and landed on the roof of their car, perfectly balanced on its rear wheel, before the man hopped the bike on to the road and raced off down the hill. The entire manoeuvre had been almost silent; the bike itself was completely electric.

Dev groaned as Lot levered the door off him. "Are you hurt? Anything broken?" she asked anxiously.

Dev shook his head. His arm was numb and a pain shot through his leg, but he didn't want to bother her with that. "Don't let him get away!" Lot raced down the steps to the car.

"What if he's left something inside?" said Aaron as Lot and Dev jumped into the front seats.

"You and Mason check it out," said Dev. His attention was drawn to the fact that Lot had taken up position behind the steering wheel.

She caught his quizzical look. "What? My dad taught me to drive on the airfield." Lot's father was an air force pilot, and Dev had no doubt that he had taught her. He was just sceptical how good she was going to be.

"There's no key!" said Lot, slamming her palms

against the wheel. "Drive!" She shouted at the car. "Go! Start engine!" The vehicle didn't respond.

Dev touched a dark display screen on the dash and focused his power. The engine instantly sprang to life. "It's all yours."

Riya had barely sat back in the car when Lot pushed the accelerator to the floor and the vehicle sprang away like a silent bullet. She yelped and twisted the wheel to avoid the parked van in front. With a clatter, her wing mirror smashed off as the side of the door scraped the paintwork of the stationary van.

"Oops! Sorry!" she yelled to the van.

"There he is!" Dev pointed down the hill to a junction just visible in the fog. The biker had stopped at a traffic light, clearly following traffic rules so as not to draw attention to himself. The lights turned green and he pulled away.

Lot gritted her teeth and weaved their car through the traffic. She didn't let up on the accelerator. The whoosh of cars passing too close seemed louder with the lack of engine noise to drown them out. In the rear, Riya gripped the back of Lot's seat, her face twisted in panic. Dev glanced at her, then patted Lot on the shoulder.

"You're doing great!" he said to Lot as they overtook

a truck — only to find themselves in the wrong lane with traffic looming straight towards them through the fog. Dozens of horns blared, catching the attention of the biker. The moment he saw them, he throttled his bike and made a sharp turn down a street.

"He's turned down there!" shouted Dev, pointing.

Lot tutted as she twisted the wheel hard. "I'm not blind!"

The electric car skidded across the junction, tyres squealing. The vehicle shuddered as she straightened out. The biker was just ahead, his lightweight engine no match for the car, which Dev had ensured was performing to its maximum capabilities.

The bike turned sharply down another street — this one a steep hill leading down to the harbour, which was lost in a grey foggy veil. The biker ramped from the top of the hill — narrowly missing a tram that was crossing the intersection. Lot wasn't so lucky.

The car was going so fast they *got air* — all four wheels lifting clear from the road. They all screamed. Lot instinctively twisted the wheel — which did nothing. Then with a loud *crump*, they struck the side of the tram.

The hood buckled and the windscreen became a mass of spiderweb cracks, completely blocking their view.

The occupants inside the tram ducked for cover as the windows on the impacted side shattered. The collision rocked the tram, forcing it off its track. The car became wedged halfway up the now-buckled side of the tram, all four wheels off the ground. The electric engine still turned all four wheels, but without the ground to resist them, they spun so fast that smoke began to rise from the rapidly overheating motor.

The cable in the road pulling the tram began to fray. The added weight of the car was just enough to cause it to snap. Free of its track, the tram began to roll, turning into the downhill slope, gaining speed with every passing second.

Dev leaned back in his seat and raised both feet to boot the broken windscreen away. The safety glass slid away like a sheet of plastic — and now they had a terrifying view ahead as they sped down the street, out of control. Just ahead, the biker was racing away from them.

The over-revving wheel motors suddenly burst into flames. Fanned by the air whipping past at speed, the tongues of fire spread to the tram. The passengers and driver leapt from the opposite side as the tram became an inferno within seconds. Thick black smoke trailed behind.

The impact had thrown the gadget satchel Mason had left on the floor into Riya's lap. She rummaged inside and pulled out a small pistol with a fat barrel. "NetGun" was etched on the side. Riya clambered to half stand in the front of the sloping car between Dev and Lot and aimed at the biker. The heat from the blazing tram was almost unbearable.

"I got him..." Riya pulled the trigger. A heavy thump of compressed air shot a spinning titanium net forward.

It expanded as it twirled straight at the biker. It hit him on the back of the head, the net folding around his head and bike. The man wobbled – then fell sideways, sliding down the road in a shower of sparks.

The bike slid to a stop at the junction at the bottom of the hill, just short of a wooden pier stretching into the bay. The tram was going too fast. It overshot the junction and bounced from the kerb so violently that Riya was tossed through the open windscreen. People walking along the waterfront screamed and fled the path of the burning tram. It screeched on to a pier, trundling across it at an angle, tearing up wooden planks in its wake.

"I think it's time we leave!" said Dev as the flames took hold of the car.

He kicked his door open and helped Lot clamber over him. She jumped without thinking. Dev followed immediately afterwards. Luckily, the tram had slowed enough so that it was no worse than jumping from a fast-moving roundabout. They both rolled several times along the ground, stopping in time to see the blazing tram and entwined car soar off the edge. There was a loud hiss of extinguished flames as it crashed into the sea.

"Well..." said Lot, catching her breath, "I'm glad we didn't end up in the water twice in one day."

Dev laughed, before remembering Riya. They ran from the damaged pier and found her standing over the biker under the net. Riya placed one foot on him to stop him from struggling.

"Victory!" she declared. "I think we're getting better at this. We hardly destroyed anything this time."

The sounds of police sirens in the fog indicated they shouldn't linger around much longer. Dev took his phone from his pocket.

"I better check if the others found anything in the house." He clicked on Mason's number, relieved that Riya was right: things could have gone a *lot* worse.

*

Mason followed Aaron into the house, pausing at the front door in time to see Lot lose a wing mirror and scrape the side of the neighbour's parked car. He sucked his teeth in sympathy for the damaged car, then entered the house.

It was immediately apparent that the house hadn't been used to live in. There was no furniture or decorations in the hallway, just a charging cable plugged into the wall that indicated the electric bike had been kept there.

"Aaron?" Mason poked his head into a room. It was completely empty. "Hey, where are you?"

He saw a line of electric cables running from sockets in the hallway, all snaking into another reception room. Mason carefully entered. In the centre of the room was a network of computers, all linked together to form a server. Several table fans were on, keeping the room cool. Aaron stood looking at Mason with an unreadable expression.

"What's the matter?" asked Mason. "We found it."

He realized that Aaron was actually looking *beyond* him. Mason slowly turned to see a figure stepping from behind the door.

"Hello, Mason," said the Collector, his blank eyes seeming to bore into him. "You've found me. Now what?"

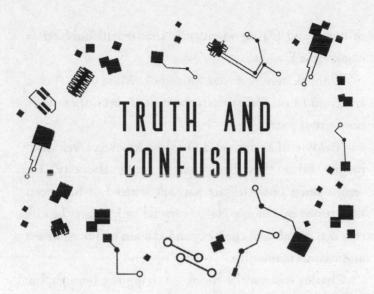

TRUTH AND CONFUSION

The Consortium had blocked off the entire street around the biker's house. The moment Dev had reported Mason and Aaron missing, Charles Parker had turned up in person with what looked like the World Consortium's entire army. Sergeant Wade was still at the Winter Tech disaster site, and Eema was tasked at the Inventory to free Onslow Winter from his amber cocoon, which was proving more difficult than anticipated. All the while, Charles was muttering about stretched resources.

Dev, Lot and Riya looked at the smouldering remains of a computer server that had sat in a back room of the house. It had melted into an acrid-smelling puddle of metal and plastic so recently that it still bubbled as smoke rose from it.

"I think whoever did this took Mase and Aaron first," said Lot. Other than the melted mess, there were no signs of a struggle.

"Baldy will know," said Dev in a low voice, referring to the biker they had chased across the city. He remembered how sick he had felt when Lot had been kidnapped by Double Helix; now he had to face the fact that one member of their expanded team had been killed and two were missing.

Charles entered the room, studying the holographic display floating over the surface of his phone. "Baldy is in fact Miles Kipthorn." He waved his hand and a soldier wearing World Consortium insignia stepped in, pulling the motocross rider from before by the elbow. His hands were tied behind his back in a seriously thick set of metal cuffs.

Charles turned to face him. "Say hello to Miles, a programmer at Winter Tech before he decided to steal secrets. Isn't that correct?"

Miles looked between them all, utterly confused. "I don't know what you're talking about." His eyes fell on the melted server. "What is that? What is this place?"

Dev knew what it was like to experience other people's thoughts; he had been carrying Tyker's around in his head for months, so he recognized genuine confusion. Miles wasn't acting.

"We chased you from here," snapped Riya. "Don't play dumb!"

"I swear I've never been here!"

Dev had expected his uncle to get angry; instead he smiled and nodded.

"Of course not. Perhaps this is all a ghastly issue of mistaken identity. Allow me to assist." Charles reached into his pocket and pulled out a small headset that unfolded with a series of clicks. Charles clamped it on to Mile's head, pressing it firmly down.

Miles struggled, but the soldier gripped both his shoulders, forcing him to stop. "What is that? Get it off me!"

"It's an old artefact we have from the fifties," said Charles amiably. "The Truth-o-Matic. It was supposed to be the ultimate lie detector. Well, it doesn't detect lies, it merely bypasses the part of your brain that forms them, so you can't." He glanced at Dev. "A little less subtle than the Lie-Pod you used, but it gets the trick done."

Dev was impressed, but also wondered how it was his uncle had never used it on him.

Charles continued talking to Miles as if they were having a pleasant Sunday afternoon conversation. "The problem, as with so many of our wonderful inventions, is that it's a little prone to crashing. And when it's plugged into your head, you don't want it to do that. Most painful."

Charles flicked a switch on the side of the machine and a blue light on the case over Miles's ear began to rhythmically flash. After a few seconds, Miles hissed in pain, closing his eyes, and the light turned green. Charles looked satisfied.

"So, Miles, you stole data from Winter Tech?"

Miles whimpered in pain, but nodded. His eyes were still tightly closed. "Yes, sir. All the files on Winter Storm. Everything. But I didn't want to do it. I was forced. . ."

"By who?"

Miles once again tried to resist, but his mouth had different ideas. "He called himself the Collector."

"Was he here?" asked Dev, before Charles could speak again.

"Yes."

"Why did you run from us?"

Miles gritted his teeth, but still the truth came. "He told me to. . ."

Dev and Lot swapped a look before Dev spoke. "He knew we'd follow you. And he'd stay behind and escape with the stolen data, correct?"

Miles shook his head, then dropped to his knees in increasing agony. He opened his bloodshot eyes, tears streaming down his face. "No . . . please take it off!"

Lot knelt down to draw level with Miles. "I can do that." She reached for the Truth-o-Matic, then stopped. "What do you mean by 'no'?"

Miles struggled not to answer. "I wasn't acting as a decoy. . . Please. Stop this. . ."

Lot exchanged a look with Riya and Dev.

Dev started to pace back and forth. "If it wasn't a decoy . . . then the Collector knew we'd split up."

"Divide and conquer," muttered Lot, remembering the phrase from a hazy history lesson.

Charles nodded. "He knows how you operate. You did the same in Marrakech. You're getting predictable."

Dev rubbed his tired eyes. "So he knew some of us would come in here. . ."

Riya took up the idea as it dawned on her too. "Whoever came back was walking into a trap!"

Tears were streaming down Miles's cheeks now. He nodded, then opened his mouth to speak again – but instead of a human voice, a high-pitched digital squeal came out. The tone modulated like a bad karaoke singer. Then a stream of bio-bots poured from the man's ears and began to attack the Truth-o-Matic.

Charles jumped several steps back in alarm, crying out: "Good Lord!"

The Consortium soldier stepped back in horror, unsure what to do. Riya reacted quickly. With a spin-kick she knocked the Truth-o-Matic from Miles's head. It clattered across the room, the bio-bots swarming after it.

"Run!" she suggested.

Charles Parker pushed past both the children and the soldier in his haste to get out. Dev and Lot each took one of Miles's arms and dragged him out. Riya gave a helping hand as they bumped him down the steps and into the street.

"Seal that place tight!" Charles yelled the moment the soldier was out of the door.

A trooper outside hurled a grenade at the house – which instantly blossomed into a giant bubble of energy around the building. The surface rippled, distorting the view inside.

Charles caught his breath. "The bio-bots are contained in there for now." He looked at Miles. "Providing there are no more in him."

Miles lay on the floor, breathing hard. "He put them in me..." he said weakly. "I couldn't stop myself ... stealing the data ... running from you. I could see it all, but it was like I was a passenger in my own body."

Lot shivered at the thought. "You were being remote controlled."

"The Collector has all the plans for Winter Storm," said Dev. "The building where it was designed and built is now lying in the sea, and the man who invented them is encased in a block of amber in the Inventory. And the Collector has taken two of our team hostage."

Lot's face hardened. "I'd say he has covered his tracks pretty well this time."

"The question is, what for?" said Charles. "Shadow Helix is leaderless. Remember Lee? He told us that."

They were hardly likely to forget him. Lee had originally broken into the Inventory with the Collector on behalf of the criminal organization Shadow Helix, only to resurface recently after defecting to an even more mysterious gang, called the Company, to chase after the Black Knight. It was an adventure that almost got them all killed – in fact, one of them had been. Wan-Soo, the Korean member of their team, who had shown his true colours as a traitor.

"And we thought the Collector was dead," Dev pointed out. "If he's not working for Helix or the Company, is he doing this alone?"

There was something nagging at Dev, the hints of a bigger, darker plan. He could see snatches of it, but the moment he tried to understand it, the thoughts and ideas disappeared like a dream. He only hoped that Aaron and Mason were safe.

They couldn't afford to lose any more members of the team.

HOW BAD CAN IT BE?

"I don't like this," said Aaron for the umpteenth time.

"You're not supposed to like it," said Mason quietly. "You're supposed to be terrified out of your tiny mind."

Aaron tutted. "Well, yeah. I *am* terrified out of my amazing mind, which is exactly why I don't like it."

They were in a plain metal room, with very little recollection of what had happened since encountering the Collector in the house. Completely unarmed, there had been little they could have done to fight the villain. Mason had a hazy memory of the fog rolling into the room, or was it a knockout gas? He had lost consciousness and woken, with Aaron, here. The beige walls curved and were welded together with thick steel rivets. Bare metal pipes emerged from one wall, crossed the ceiling and vanished into another. Other than a continuous faint hum, there were no other signs of life beyond the room. There was a single circular door with a wheel lock in the centre.

"Do you know what this reminds me of?" asked Aaron, desperate not to be left in silence.

"A boat," said Mason, putting all his strength into turning the wheel. It didn't budge. "I've been on one before with the Collector."

"I was going to say submarine, actually," said Aaron. After a thoughtful pause, he asked: "What happened on the boat?"

"Oh, it got wrecked. Badly. I've been on a sub too."

Aaron's tone dropped as he anticipated the answer to his next question. "And what happened to that?"

"Crashed it." Mason strained to open the door again.

"I'm noticing a pattern."

Mason gave up on the door and walked in a circle, eying the ceiling for any cameras. "Mmm. It usually involves explosions. Lots of screaming. Something really bad happening. Then silence."

"That's not very reassuring." Aaron folded his arms, but his right leg shook restlessly. "Why aren't you panicking about all of this?"

Mason stopped his inspection and looked at Aaron with a half grin. "Because this is what we do, right? I used to be like you. Terrified of everything. Now I just sit back and go with the flow."

"That's your plan for getting us out of here? Sit back and see what happens?"

"No," he said slowly. "Not entirely. I also plan to work out where *here* is. Then work out if it's worth escaping from."

"Worth escaping from? You mean in case this is a fun prison?"

"If the Collector wanted us dead, he wouldn't have wasted his time bringing us here."

"That doesn't sound as reassuring as you think it does."

Mason shrugged. "Try and relax. Things are never as bad as you think."

With a clang, the door's wheel lock suddenly spun around. Then the heavy door swung open with a dull thump that reverberated around the room.

"I hope this is room service," Mason quipped,

determined not to show any fear. "I'm starving." His grin slid from his face when he saw who had opened the door. Now he was confused.

"Never as bad, huh?" said Aaron, his face turning pale. "I'd hate to see what you think is bad. . ."

DEAD
SILENCE

Dev felt a little reassured when they boarded the
Avrocar. His uncle had arrived in San Francisco in it,
flying in with a fleet of other aircraft, and now they
were returning to the Inventory together.

Dev took his seat next to Lot and felt painfully aware
of Mason and Aaron's absence. Where were they now?
Were they even alive?

Charles Parker was sitting in Aaron's seat. He had
made sure Miles had been secured aboard one of the
VTOL aircrafts that was escorting them back.

"It'll be just a few minutes in this thing, right?"
said Dev with a yawn. The stress of the day was eating

his strength and he wanted nothing more than to sleep.

"We are escorting the other aircraft. Miles is an important piece of evidence," said Charles as they took off in formation.

Dev ignored the fact his uncle was referring to a fellow human as a mere item. He was used to it; Dev always felt that Charles treated him as just another object in the Inventory.

"We need to see what damage the bio-bots did to him," Charles added. "It may show clues to their weaknesses. We can't afford the Collector launching an attack to destroy the only loose end he left." He got up and went to the back of the cabin with his phone, trying unsuccessfully to track down Sergeant Wade.

Dev talked low to Lot. "Have you ever wondered what would happen if you told your parents about all of this?"

"They would probably think it was awesome," said Lot. She flashed her smile, which always made Dev smile in turn, no matter how bad a mood he was in.

"You don't think they would ask you to stop because it's too dangerous?"

Lot thought about that for a moment, her smile fading. "Probably. You know how parents can be..."

The words were out of her mouth before she realized. "Dev, I'm sorry. I didn't mean. . ."

He gently patted her hand. "It's OK. I know you didn't." After a thoughtful pause, he added, "Before all of this, all of the missions, I often wondered what had happened to my parents." He indicated to Charles. "He made me. Used some of his own DNA, so that makes him 'dad'." Lot smiled when Dev made the air quotes with his fingers. "But I must have had a mum, right? I mean . . . even if only partly. . ."

He shook his head and gazed at the floor. The rest of the journey passed in silence. Riya had stretched back, listening to music on her phone while Lot had fallen asleep, her head rolling on to Dev's shoulder. He was too afraid of waking her if he pushed her away. Plus, it felt comforting to have somebody to lean on.

Dev closed his eyes, but no matter how tired he felt, his mind was too active to sleep. Thoughts of what had happened in the Black Zone bounced through his mind. They were quickly overtaken by the vision of Tyker falling into the mass of bio-bots. In his mind's eye his imagination filled in the details in ultra-high definition. The look of fear on Tyker's face was a chilling sight.

Dev was just drifting in the zone between sleep and wakefulness when he felt someone tap his shoulder. His eyes flicked open and saw Charles standing over him, placing his fingers to his lips to indicate they stay quiet. Lot had shifted away from Dev and was now curled up in her seat, fast asleep. In the row behind, Riya was likewise down for the count.

"What is it?" whispered Dev, his eyes straying to the controls; he was already anticipating danger. The other aircraft were flying in formation around them, and they were steadily approaching Inventory airspace. But nothing seemed amiss.

"Do you know what an ILS is?" asked Charles quietly. Dev could see his uncle's face was creased with new lines of worry.

Dev shook his head.

"The Instrument Landing System. An automated signal that tells the aircraft where to land if they can't see the runway. A good pilot can land using ILS without ever needing to see outside."

"So?" said Dev, confused.

"We're not picking up the Inventory's ILS. Can you check whether the Avro is malfunctioning?"

Dev looked at the screen. It was a clear day outside;

he couldn't imagine why his uncle thought they needed the ILS to land. With a sigh that came naturally to every teenager being asked to wash the dishes or save the world, Dev laid his palm against the control panel. His synaesthesia spoke to the system, and he could suddenly sense every aspect of the Avrocar as if it was his own body. A malfunctioning sensor or piece of equipment would be as telltale as if he had cut himself.

"Nope. She's working just fine." Dev patted the control panel, thankful that nothing else was going wrong that day. "Anyway, we don't need the ILS. We've landed this thing by sight, and skill, loads of times. Well, Lot has," he added, glancing at her.

Charles quickly checked the girls were asleep before speaking again.

"Then that means the ILS system in the Inventory is down. It never breaks. Never. We have a dozen backups."

"What does Ecma say about it?"

"That's the other concern..." Charles left the words hanging.

"The radio's working fine," said Dev.

They both turned to the view on the panoramic display screens. The landscape ahead was familiar. They were closing in on the Inventory.

"I have a bad feeling about this," Dev muttered as he reached for the control panel again.

The noise from the cutting laser sounded like a dentist's drill and set Sergeant Wade's teeth on edge. The multi-jointed robotic arm carefully drew the laser back and forth over the amber material encasing Onslow Winter. The process had already taken close to an hour and Wade was becoming increasingly bored. However, the casing around Winter had been formed from a small cube into a snug human-sized form now only millimetres thick, so it looked as if Winter had amber-coloured skin.

"Eema, how are his vital signs?" asked Wade, her eyes transfixed on the swooping laser cutter.

"Stable. Winter is in a state of deep sleep," came Eema's voice from the computer. The spherical husk that was the computer's physical body was elsewhere in the Inventory. "When the case around him cracks open, the oxygen in the atmosphere should revive him."

The laser cutter pirouetted around Winter's cheek-bones and forehead before neatly carving the covering away under his chin. The amber mask slid from his face and shattered on the floor. The moment it fell, Winter automatically sucked in a deep breath as if emerging from the deep ocean. His chest expanded, cracking the casing like ice.

Wade leaned forward and pulled broken pieces from his face. "Onslow, can you hear me? You're safe. I'm here to help you."

Winter's lips were cracked and dry. He tried to say something, but it came out as a croak. Then he smiled weakly. Wade frowned as the veins in the man's neck suddenly turned black. She reached out to him, but then pulled her hand back as two lumps on his forehead formed like horns — and a stream of bio-bots poured out from his head, circling Wade like a swarm of bees.

Dev felt his synaesthesia prod the Avro's communications systems. They responded as if they were an itch in his palm. In his mind's eye, he could see the ship's sensors capturing data from the ground below — everything from phone signals that appeared as a mass of colourful waving ribbons through to TV channels. Everything was working fine — except the special radio channel reserved for Inventory coms was completely dead. Just a blank space where it was supposed to be.

"I'm picking up dead silence on the IVX channel," Dev said with growing concern. "Not even static."

Lot shifted in her chair next to him and sleepily yawned. "Are we nearly there?" The lack of a reply and the furrowed brows of Dev and Charles focused her senses. "What's happened?"

"We can't get through to the Inventory," said Dev as he double-checked the Avro's sensors. "Everything is working on this side."

Charles sighed as he shook his phone in frustration. "I can't get through to Wade either. Lot, take over from the autopilot. Circle us around. If they don't know we're coming, they can't open the hangar doors."

Lot sprang upright in her seat, glad to be asked. Although the Inventory engineers had told her she was the best Avro pilot they'd ever known, she didn't think Charles would trust her over the autopilot technology.

The control stick morphed from the console in front of her, sliding effortlessly into her outstretched hands. On contact with her palms, the aircraft turned its autopilot off and Lot positioned them in a wide circular orbit around the farm far below. Their convoy of aircraft followed suit.

*

"So, do you want to tell us what is going on?" said Mason as he and Aaron were escorted down the corridor. When no reply was forthcoming from their mechanical guard, he leaned closer to Aaron and spoke in a whisper. "Do you remember what happened in San Fran?"

"Not after we saw that dude with the weird eyes. Who was he?"

"The Collector. The Inventory's Most Wanted ... or he was before we destroyed him and his hoodlums. Before your time."

"He's a bad guy. Got it."

"The baddest. Which is why I'm asking you if you remember anything. Like us being rescued."

Aaron shook his head. "Nope. And I would say there's nothing about this that feels normal. Or what passes for normal around here."

They reached a door and their guard spun around to face them.

"I have no wish to restrain you, so when we pass through here, behave. Or it won't be restraints. I'll terminate you."

The door slid open. Mason gulped. He had no doubt their guard would kill them without a second thought. After all, it was a guard he thought he knew very well.

He stared long and hard into the hovering red emoji face and nodded.

"I promise, Eema," he said. "You'll have no funny business from us."

Dev's head snapped up to the screen when an incoming message flashed up. Before they could question who it was from, a video feed appeared.

"Good evening, Charles," said the Collector.

Dev felt his blood run cold. He glanced at his uncle and saw him tense. He opened his mouth to speak, but his reply came out as nothing more than a stammering sound.

The Collector appeared pleased with the response. "I will cut to the chase, as they say. As you may have suspected, I am calling from your home. The heart of the Inventory."

Dev couldn't restrain the gasp of shock that escaped his lips.

"After all the fuss in getting in here last time, this time I made it simple. All I needed was a Trojan horse. But enough about *my* genius. I have full control here. And I have hostages to ensure you don't do something stupid."

The camera widened out to show Mason and Aaron standing in front of a red-headed Eema. Dev recognized the room as the Inventory's main control bunker.

The Collector smiled. "You won't hear from me again. I have no list of demands, Charles. I just wanted you to see that I have won." The camera image slowly zoomed back to the fiend's face. "I'm sorry it went this way, Dev. But as my replacement, you could still never best me. I'm afraid the last sound you will hear will be the screech of alarms as the targeted missiles I am about to launch lock on to you. Goodbye, dear family."

The image vanished.

Nobody spoke. Then Riya woke up and yawned.

"Hey, guys. What did I miss?"

On the screen, they could see four flashes from below as the Collector turned the Inventory's own defences on them. Alarms suddenly shrieked across the cabin, and the ship's computer spoke up in a chillingly calm voice.

"Missile lock detected."

EVASIVE MANOEUVRES

Every one of Lot's senses screamed *run*. That translated into her pushing the Avro into a sharp banking manoeuvre so that it plummeted earthward. The ship's artificial gravity was all that kept their feet on the floor or they would have probably blacked out due to the intense G-forces.

The nearest incoming missile sharply arced to follow their new trajectory, and it zoomed past their aircraft so close that it momentarily filled the viewing screen. A second later it detonated. The force of the explosion shook the Avro fiercely, and the clatter of shrapnel rattled across the hull. Even more alarms sounded in the cabin.

"We've taken damage," said Dev as the sensors reported back to him through his synaesthesia. A warm prickling in his left arm told him what was wrong. "The stealth processor has been damaged. Everyone can see us."

"Another missile is on our tail!" yelled Lot, whose eyes were glued to the instruments.

"Let it get close again," said Dev. Lot levelled the Avro out.

"No!" Charles snapped. "These are adaptive missile defences." He noticed their blank looks and shook his head. "I don't have time to ... never mind. Whatever actions you do won't work on the next missile. They learn."

"Oh great," sighed Riya. "A missile that learns. Like the world needed that."

"It's wonderful ... if it's *defending* you," said Charles, instinctively gripping the console in front of him as Lot banked the Avro first left, then sharply right. The missile thundered past but didn't detonate. Instead it kept on its path.

"Oh no. . ." said Lot as she realized what was about to happen.

The missile struck the Osprey carrying Miles. They

all watched helplessly as a wing tore off, sending the aircraft spiralling to the fields below.

"There's another one!" screamed Riya, pointing to a different part of the display window.

Dev tore his gaze from the stricken Osprey as the third missile fell in behind them.

"I've got this!" he roared with a snarl of anger. His powers snatched the controls from Lot and he brought the leading edge of the Avro up. The aircraft flipped like a spinning coin — allowing the missile to pass harmlessly underneath while the Avro accelerated in the opposite direction.

Riya stood from her seat behind and whooped. "Nice move!"

Dev's sense of pride was toppled moments later when Lot spoke up.

"It's pulled a U-turn. It's back on our tail!"

Dev glanced at the rear monitor and saw the projectile was zeroing in on them. Just as he considered performing the same move, it suddenly broke apart into dozens of smaller missiles that spread out like a cloud. Dev stopped himself performing the manoeuvre just in time — had he done so, he would have flipped the Avro straight into the missiles.

"I told you they learn!" said Charles. "We don't stand a chance up here. The Inventory has scores of defences." Charles gripped Dev's arm, forcing him to look at him. "We have get out of here."

Dev saw the hurt in his uncle's eyes. He suspected that losing his precious artefacts was something worse than if he lost Dev. Losing the entire Inventory, that was another matter. He glanced at the monitor and saw the Osprey had crashed in a field, leaving a half-mile-long trench behind it. The plane was on fire, but as he willed the camera to zoom in, he could see the crew were running from the wreckage.

Dev was so torn in his decision that he had taken his focus off the missile for far too long.

"Impact!" screamed Lot.

Dev's synaesthesia reacted faster than his flesh and muscles could. He thrust the Avro into a steep climb a split second later – just as the dozens of miniature missiles detonated. The shock wave rattled the Avro, and Dev felt stabbing pains across his body as his gift reported on the damage the hull was sustaining...

And like a physical punch to his gut, the artificial gravity generator was struck by shrapnel. Since they were no longer being pulled straight down to the deck, the rest of the world's physics kicked into action. Lot and Dev were pushed into their seats as the aircraft climbed vertically upward.

Riya screamed as she was hurled off her feet and back in the seat. Charles, who had been standing next to Dev, was thrown to the back of the cabin with such force they heard the interior wall crack.

Dev pulled the Avro level and tried to engage the autopilot. It failed to activate; that too was damaged.

"Charles?" he called out. His uncle didn't move. "Uncle? Lot, take the controls."

Lot once again took the stick and Dev ran to the back of the cabin, pausing only slightly to check Riya was unhurt. She was clutching her right arm.

"I think it's broken," she said through the pain.

"Put your seat belt on." Dev hurried to his uncle's side. Charles was lying on the floor, a nasty cut on his forehead. He wasn't moving. The bulkhead he had struck was dented from the impact, and Dev was sure his uncle must have several broken bones. Dev felt for a pulse – it was there, but weak.

It suddenly struck him that he didn't know what to do.

All his life he had complained that Charles Parker

didn't care about what he wanted. Didn't care if Dev knew the truth or was thrust into life-threatening danger. When Dev learned the truth that he was a clone, he had resented his "uncle" further. But every time Dev had come back from the mission – or, as he suspected, his mind had, if not his body – his uncle had seen to it, albeit from a distance, that Dev had been looked after. And now, with the tables turned and his uncle in need of help, he had no idea what to do.

"The last missile has locked on to us!" shouted Lot, her voice breaking with panic. "Hold on!"

Dev didn't have time to move before she threw the Avro into a sharp dive earthward. He was plucked off his feet and spun in the sudden zero gravity. His uncle's body floated past him and gently thumped against the ceiling. Dev knew they only had seconds of weightlessness before Lot had to pull them out of the dive. He only had seconds to secure his frail uncle before the next impact killed him.

Dev kicked out against a wall – propelling himself towards Charles. Luckily, his experience on board the Black Knight had prepared him for working in zero G, and his aim was perfect. He landed – upside down – on the roof, next to his uncle. He wrapped his arms around

Charles's waist and, with a slight bend of the knees, thrust them both towards the seats next to Riya.

Out of the corner of his eye, Dev could see the ground was looming — filling the viewport screen. Desperate, he pushed Charles across both seats. Riya reached across with her good arm and helped Dev lock both seat belts over Charles. Dev somersaulted over the bank of seats, and no sooner had his bum lightly touched his own seat than Lot yanked the stick to pull the Avro from its dive.

The G-force was so incredible they all felt the crushing weight on their chests and they blacked out.

Dev blinked in surprise — unaware if he had been unconscious for a second or longer. Lot was still out, her hand gripping the stick as they levelled out over a copse of trees. The clatter of the topmost branches scraping across the hull could be heard a moment before the pursuing missile ploughed into the trees, incinerating them in a hellish fireball.

Lot woke with a start — and renewed her grip on the controls. It took her a few more seconds to work out what was going on.

"We did it!" she exclaimed. "We beat the missile defences!"

Then the ship's automatic voice piped up. "Warning, missile launches detected."

On the monitors, they could see another four rockets had been sent after them.

Dev sighed. "Lot, get us out of here." She met his gaze and saw the concern in his eyes. "Far away. We have to get my uncle to a hospital."

Lot nodded and wordlessly activated the hypersonic engines.

"Hold on," she warned — and throttled them up to full speed.

IN THE COMPANY OF STRANGERS

The Avro was almost impossible to fly after sustaining so much damage. It took all of Lot's concentration and talent to stop the aircraft breaking up at hypersonic speeds, a task usually given to the now-malfunctioning autopilot. Dev wanted to check on his uncle's condition but was forced to wade in with his synaesthesia to help Lot keep control.

Riya used her jacket to form a crude sling before turning her attention to Charles Parker. She detected his feeble pulse, but his breathing remained shallow.

"We need to find the nearest hospital," she said in a calm but urgent voice. "We can't wait much longer."

When Dev judged they were an appropriate distance from the Inventory, they slowed the Avro back into regular flight mode. The viewing screens revealed they were close to a coastal city. Lights shone below like a spiderweb pushed against the utter black of the ocean. They could feel a strong wind buffet the aircraft as Lot struggled to make it hover. The pelt of heavy rain on the hull added to the sense of despair they were all feeling.

Dev called up a map of the area. The screen remained blank. He rolled his eyes and thumped the controls.

"We've lost all connectivity with the Inventory," he said, rubbing his eyes. "We're flying blind. We could be anywhere!"

"We're over Boston, USA," Riya said. Lot and Dev looked curiously at her. Riya held up her precious mobile phone. "I've got a signal up here! And according to the internet ... the best hospital here is the Massachusetts General Hospital."

Using Riya's map app, Lot guided the Avro down to the hospital. At slow speeds the aircraft was even less responsive.

Dev's eyes were glued to the screen as they swayed over the hospital's car park. "Remember, we don't have any camouflage. Anybody can see us."

Lot bit her lower lip in concentration. "I don't think that matters. This is not going to be a subtle landing."

The Avro swayed to and fro in the wind as Lot lowered them towards the full car park. It was a little after ten p.m., so the night shift was beginning to get busy with two ambulances arriving at the ER.

Dev used his power to activate the landing gear. The response he received didn't fill him with joy.

"Um, would you believe the landing gear is damaged."

"I can't see any place to land," said Riya, searching for a clear area below.

"This will do," said Lot quietly as she brought the Avro in low – then suddenly cut the engines.

A dozen people stood outside the hospital, braving the driving rain. They looked up to see the flying saucer drop on to several parked cars. The vehicles folded under the saucer's weight, their car alarms screeching.

By the time the spectators edged forward, wiping rain from their glasses or using their hands to shield their eyes, the disc had come to a rest at a slight angle with its hatch open and a ramp extended, not quite reaching the ground.

The onlookers were so fascinated that nobody paid

any attention to the three children entering the hospital, carrying an older man between them.

Dev yawned and shuffled his bum in the uncomfortable plastic chair. They had been in the waiting room for almost two hours and watched a tide of drunks, people sporting nasty wounds from fights and one man who inexplicably had a plastic bucket wedged over his head. Lot was asleep, her head yet again on Dev's shoulder.

He was almost reluctant to wake her when Riya appeared with her forearm in a cast. She grinned and held it up.

"Broken in two places!" she said proudly. "Any word on your uncle?"

Dev nodded towards a group of nurses conferring at the reception desk. "They said he was still unconscious and were waiting for an MRI scan."

"What did you tell them had happened?"

Lot stretched and yawned as she answered. "Said he was in a car crash. I don't know if you've looked outside, but I don't think telling them how we got here is a good idea."

Riya peeked out of the waiting room doors. The car park was filled with police vehicles and a couple of military trucks circling the Avro. A huge crowd had gathered, but armed soldiers were keeping them at bay. News reporters were beginning to arrive, broadcasting live to the world.

"I think we've lost the Avro," Lot sighed.

Riya pointed to the aircraft. "Don't you think that's a big clue if the bad guys want to track us down? I mean, all the Collector has to do is turn on the TV and he can find us."

"True," said Dev. "But he has spent all this time trying to get into the Inventory. I doubt very much he's just going to pop out to find us. What's the point? I'm hoping that Wade has seen the reports and is heading over."

He didn't want to admit it, but worry was gnawing at him. No matter how bad things got on a mission, they always had his uncle, Eema, the Inventory staff and Sergeant Wade backing them up. And right now, they had no support. They were on their own. He was surprised Wade hadn't turned up; she surely must know about the Inventory breach by now? And the fact the team were missing . . . yet she hadn't showed.

That was another worry. What had happened to her?

Riya looked thoughtful. "If the Collector is in the Inventory . . . he still can't get anything out." She looked at Dev. "You're the security key. You're the real Iron Fist, remember, not that battle mech."

The new recruits had been briefed on Dev's role as a genetically modified living key that prevented items from being taken out of the Inventory. When the Collector had first attacked, he had lured Dev through the only escape route out of the underground maze, thus deactivating the security and allowing him to perform the largest heist in history. But without Dev, the tech would self-destruct the moment it was taken out.

"Unless the security system had been taken offline," mused Lot. "I mean, who could do that?" She stopped herself when she noticed a man looking over at them. Dressed in a tweed three-piece suit, with immaculately groomed hair, he leaned on a black cane, managing to look completely out of place in the busy hospital. She nudged Dev, then nodded over towards him.

"He's staring at us," she mumbled.

The man crossed purposefully towards them. Dev tensed, his eyes darting to the exit, but there was little point in running. They had nowhere to go.

Then, to his surprise, the man stopped in front of

him and said in a perfect British accent, "Devon Parker, good lord."

Dev frowned. "Do I know you?"

The man carefully looked at Lot and Riya, before turning his attention back to Dev.

"No. But you should. You are all in terrific danger."

"What's so terrific about it?" Riya asked, confused.

"Terrific as in terrible, great."

"From you?" she asked with an edge in her voice that warned the man a fight was coming should he try anything.

The man gave her a thin smile. "My dear lady, I wouldn't dream of it." He turned to Dev. "But I don't think Charles Parker will be safe for much longer."

A chill ran through Dev. Without thinking, he charged down the corridor, running past the admin desk. The nurses gathered there looked up, and one reached out to stop him.

"Hey! You can't—!"

But they were shoved aside as Riya and Lot followed, the Suited Man huffing and puffing several metres behind.

The long white corridors all looked the same, and the signs pointing the way had been abbreviated to the point of being unintelligible: ENT, CCU, MOB ... nothing appeared to say MRI. Dev stopped at a junction and looked around helplessly. Riya and Lot caught up with him.

"The MRI's like an X-ray, isn't it?" said Lot.

"Not quite," said Dev, racking his brain. "It stands for Magnetic ... something ... Image... I can't remember."

"Magnetic Resonance Imaging," said the Suited Man, catching them up and already out of breath. "And it's that way." He pointed his walking stick down a corridor.

Dev was unsure whether to trust the man, but couldn't fathom why he would warn them about Charles one minute and lead them the wrong way the next.

"You four! Stay right there!" came the deep voice of a security guard running towards them.

"Go," said the Suited Man in a soft voice, before turning towards the guard. "Is there a problem, officer?"

Dev, Lot and Riya followed the directions, glancing back in time to see the Suited Man's cane strike the guard's legs. There was a flash of light and the guard crumpled to the floor.

"There!" said Riya, pointing to a door ahead that bore the sign MRI.

Dev shouldered through the door at speed, skidding

to a halt inside the new room. It looked just like any other plain, white medical room. A pair of technicians stood behind a glass screen in a booth against one wall, regarding Dev with surprise.

An aggressively loud metallic thumping made Dev spin around. It was coming from the MRI – a large circular machine covered in smooth white panels. His uncle lay on a flat table that was slowly moving through a hole in the centre of the machine.

Lot and Riya entered the room seconds later, prompting a technician to furiously wave his arms and yell at them. From behind the glass, and drowned out by the rhythmic hammering from the machine, they couldn't hear a word, but the meaning was obvious: *get out!*

Dev was unsure what to do. There was no clear threat to his uncle and the MRI procedure was necessary to treat him. He took one step backwards before he noticed a strand of smoke spiralling down from a plastic ventilation grid in the ceiling. Its movements were unnatural, almost snake-like.

By the time the Suited Man had caught up with them, it was clearly not smoke but bio-bots falling to the ground and forming the perfect shape of a smooth grey muscular figure: Winter Storm, the same menace that had pursued them in Marrakech.

Without thinking, Dev took a step to block its path to his uncle. He felt a sudden tug on his jacket and a strong pull towards the MRI machine. His trainers squeaked across the floor as he was hauled backwards by an invisible force. He leaned forward to stop himself and glanced behind.

The bottom of his jacket was almost horizontal as it was drawn towards the machine. He noticed he had crossed a yellow line on the floor and immediately realized the mistake he had made. The MRI had powerful magnets inside, so powerful they could pull metal implants out of a patient with the force of a bullet. His phone and the jacket's metal zipper were now being tugged towards the machine.

The Winter Storm seized on Dev's immobility and stepped closer. Dev relaxed his arms — and his jacket was dragged from him and thudded against the side of the MRI. No longer pulled backwards, he toppled to his knees just as Winter Storm attempted to grab him.

The bio-bot tripped over Dev and went sprawling towards the MRI.

Dev yelled victoriously. "HA!"

He had expected Winter Storm to be pulled towards the MRI and pinned in place once it crossed the line. Instead, it just caught its balance and turned to face Dev. It was completely unaffected by the MRI. Lot must have been thinking the same as Dev, but reached the facts sooner.

"It's a bio-bot! It's not metal!" She grabbed a nearby wooden chair and slung it at Winter Storm. The wood splintered across it, but did little else to slow it down.

Winter Storm appeared to study Dev, then turned back to Charles Parker lying motionless in the heart of the MRI. It strode towards him, raising an arm. Dev watched in horror as its arm transformed to a huge spike. The intention was clear – Winter Storm was going to kill Charles Parker.

And Dev and the others had no way to stop it.

UNSTOPPABLE

Ignoring the thumping MRI machine, Winter Storm leaned on it with one hand and raised its wicked spiked arm. Dev wondered why the technicians had left the MRI running with everybody in the room, but a quick glance through the control booth's window showed both men were watching the events with open mouths.

Then an idea struck Dev. He sprinted towards the MRI, dropping to the floor and skidding across the smooth tiles before his momentum gently shunted him against the machine. The sudden movement gave Winter Storm a moment's distraction from Charles Parker.

It was all Dev needed. He ducked around the

back of the MRI and shoved both hands against the machine.

"RUN!" he roared.

Lot got the message and shoved Riya from the room — the both of them cannoning into the Suited Man standing behind them.

With no time to spare, Dev couldn't check they were out of the room. He surged his synaesthesia into the MRI. Every muscle in his body ached as he pressed against the machine and every nerve hurt as he forced the machine into overload. The magnets reacted instantly as the current through them increased.

For a moment, nothing happened except the alarms in the control room broke the two men from their daze. They stabbed buttons on the console to no avail; Dev had control of the machine now. Then with a screech, metal items from the control room lifted free and clattered against the glass.

Dev increased the charge further.

The technicians had the presence of mind to flee through a door in the back of the booth, just as the observation window shattered as the metal items pressing against it shot through like darts.

It sounded like a hail of ricocheting bullets as the

metal debris struck both Winter Storm and the MRI. Dev was shielded behind the machine and could only hope nothing struck his uncle.

With a crunch, the door to the room was pulled off its metal hinges. The wood shattered across Winter Storm with enough force to knock it off balance. With another loud clang, the MRI control desk was lifted by the increased magnetic force and soared across the room. It struck Winter Storm so hard that its arm was torn off in a cloud of bio-bots that scattered across the room like ball bearings.

Out in the corridor, Lot, Riya and the Suited Man felt the powerful magnetic tug pull at their clothing. Other nurses and orderlies in the corridor felt it too. One woman was wrestling her own arm as her watch was pulled towards the room. Two gurneys sped between Lot and Riya, moving so fast they were almost knocked off their feet.

Then a loud screeching sound resonated down the hallway. Lot looked around for the source of the sound...

As did Dev, who could just hear it above the frantic knocking from the MRI's magnets. Smoke was rising from the machine now, and he could feel the heat singeing the palms of his hands, but he didn't dare let go.

Winter Storm stepped around the side of the MRI. A stream of bio-bots from its severed arm flowed into its foot, feeding a rapidly re-forming new arm – which slowly extended towards Dev.

At that moment, with a terrible screech, the roof gave way.

The metal girders supporting the room snapped as their bolts sheared under the intense magnetic wave. A huge girder slammed into Winter Storm, tearing the bio-bot swarm in half – both of which wobbled before cascading to the floor in a pile of micro parts, unable to hold together.

Then with a mighty thud, a huge piece of metal machinery was pulled through the ceiling. It struck the MRI with such force there was an explosion. Dev was hurled into the wall – the magnets instantly powering down the moment he lost contact with the machine. Metal debris noisily clattered from the MRI as they fell to the floor. The room began to fill with smoke as the fire licked the walls.

Dev crawled to the machine and saw his uncle was still cocooned in the middle of the MRI. By some miracle, the machine had taken the brunt of the impact.

"Dev!" yelled Lot from the doorway. She looked relieved to see him unharmed.

"Get a stretcher!" he yelled back.

Riya and the Suited Man were already pushing a gurney into the room. Everybody was coughing because of the smoke. The man held a handkerchief over his mouth, but his eyes were streaming.

Through the smoke, Dev could just make out the bio-bots re-forming as they poured from the debris. Hitting, burning and magnetism had failed to stop them. Dev had a horrible feeling nothing would.

Together they lifted Charles Parker out of the MRI. Fortunately, he was lying on a movable mattress that slid on to the gurney, so they couldn't harm him any further. As Winter Storm slowly reassembled in the smoke behind, Dev and Co. raced Charles Parker into the corridor — just as the fire alarm rang.

Riya coughed, her voice hoarse from the smoke. "How are we going to get away from that thing?"

"I can help you, if you allow me," said the Suited Man.

Dev rubbed his bloodshot eyes. "Who are you?"

The stranger extended his hand. Dev automatically reached out to shake it, but the man was only stretching his arm so he could look at his watch. He placed a finger on a dial and looked Dev in the eye.

"That can wait. The question is, do you want to live?"

The screech of twisted metal from the room behind indicated Winter Storm had reassembled. They heard the pounding of footsteps as it ran through the smoke towards them.

"I want to live," said Riya urgently.

Dev nodded. The man smiled and twisted the dial on his watch – just as Winter Storm charged into the room like a rampaging bull.

THE
TAKEOVER

"I feel like I'm having déjà vu," Mason said, leaning close to Aaron. They were in the Green Zone, where the shelves reached several storeys tall and stretched into the distance. There were still a lot of gaps where the Collector had plundered the Inventory previously, but now, after many retrieval trips around the globe, there weren't nearly as many.

"Except last time we were here, I was pursuing you," said the Collector. Eema rolled further back behind them, her holo-head still burning a malevolent red.

"We beat you then, we'll beat you again," Mason snorted defiantly.

The Collector stopped in his tracks so suddenly that Mason almost walked into him. The villain slowly turned, his blank eyes still managing to bore into Mason's soul. "Times have changed, Mason." The Collector gestured around. "All of this is mine now. No Devon, no Charles Parker, no Lottie . . . only you two."

Where there should have been teams of Inventory technicians going about their business, there were now mean-looking troopers wearing heavy combat armour, their faces hidden behind black masks. The few technicians on the floor appeared pale and frightened, and they looked away when they saw the Collector coming through.

"Any time you want to open the doors and let us go. . ." Mason hinted.

The Collector's hollow laugh echoed around the zone. "But you are needed here."

"It's nice to be wanted," said Aaron.

The Collector turned to Aaron. "You, not so much."

Aaron blanched.

Mason watched as Eema circled around to face him. "Any time you want to stop acting weird, feel free to jump in and help."

The Collector patted Eema. "She won't be rushing to

your aid this time. She never had a chance to lock her personality away in a safe place like last time. Onslow Winter's bio-bots are inside her now. Etched into her brain like a permanent infection. Your dear old Eema is nothing more than a war machine now."

Mason felt sorry for the old robot. She was technically nothing more than a super-smart computer program, but she had a personality; she was a person, of a sort. Although her sarcastic comments had usually annoyed him, he now found that he missed them.

"Where is Winter now?" asked Aaron.

"He is here. Recuperating."

Aaron tilted his head defiantly. "He won't like you messing with his creations. Winter is a genius. He'll figure a way to bring you down."

The Collector pointed at Aaron. "You are most irritating. I think I shall have Eema disintegrate you first."

With a swish of metal, a concealed panel on Eema's body opened up and an arm unfurled like an octopus tentacle, on the end of which a fist-sized barrel began to glow with a steady green light that bounced back and forth with increasing speed and a rising hum.

The Collector sniggered at Aaron, who was frozen

to the spot. Even the nearest shelves were too far to seek cover once Eema open fired.

"But not yet."

Eema's arm recoiled into her shell.

"The downside of her reprogramming is that several memory banks were destroyed. An unfortunate side effect, as they would have been very useful in my current search. So you two are going to help me."

Now Mason laughed. "Wait a second. We've been through all of this before. You stole a whole bunch of this weird tech and, in case it escaped your weird eyes, you don't have Iron Fist."

Iron Fist was the unique security system that ensured objects couldn't be taken outside the Inventory unless it had been properly deactivated by a "key" — and that came in the form of a person: Dev.

Mason continued. "And although you tricked him last time, it won't happen again."

The Collector tutted loudly. "This time we are not looking for a *thing*. We are looking for a *place*."

OLD RIVALS

Riya leaned closer to the window. "That is a cool view."

Ordinarily Dev would have agreed, but instead he merely grunted and shuffled in the green-leather wingback chair he had been sitting in for the last thirty minutes.

Lot was still prowling the oak-panelled room, examining every drawer and cupboard in the old wooden cabinetry that lined the walls. She had spent several minutes prodding and pushing the components of a huge ornate grandfather clock that marked the passage of time with a heavy *tick-tock*, before declaring it to be a real clock.

One moment they had been facing Winter Storm as it charged from the smoke, the bio-bots still assembling with every step it took. Then the Suited Man had twisted the dial on his watch and the effect had been instantaneous: there was a fierce yellow light and a single rising tone. They had all felt as if they were being stretched like gum. Lot had sworn she'd had an out-of-body experience and was looking down on her own head before the rest of her body snapped to catch her up. It was a sickening experience, but it was over in seconds as it reversed. The tone lowered to a bass note and their bodies felt squished. As the light faded, they found themselves in this room.

Three doctors had been waiting for them, dressed in immaculate whites, their faces covered by masks. They immediately wheeled Charles Parker from the room, the Suited Man close behind. Before Dev could follow, a thick wooden door slammed in his face. A quick check confirmed they had been locked inside.

No amount of shouldering the door would open it. Riya had tried to open the large windows and, when that hadn't worked, had attempted to hurl a chair through them. But it had bounced from the glass and almost knocked her out. She didn't try that again.

Dev had probed the room with his synaesthesia and found no electronics, except the lights, which were charged by solar panels stuck to the windows. That created a closed loop, so there was nowhere for him to extend his powers.

Frustrated, he had eventually sat down and tried to put everything together. Riya was now enjoying a view of Tower Bridge, the majestic bascule bridge that crossed London's River Thames. At least they knew where they were. Occasional glances at the grandfather clock showed an hour had crawled past since they had arrived.

Nobody made a move when the door eventually opened and the Suited Man entered, followed by a butler pushing a tea tray, filled with sandwiches, biscuits and an assortment of Cokes, lemonades and fruit juices.

"So sorry to keep you waiting," he said, motioning the butler to leave the room. He waited until the door was closed before continuing. "Please: eat, drink. You must be hungry."

Lot and Riya took handfuls of sandwiches. Lot managed to shove a whole triangle in her mouth in a single attempt. Dev wasn't feeling hungry, so remained seated.

The man positioned himself to face Dev. "Your uncle is in stable condition and is being treated by our very best medics." Dev silently nodded his thanks. "You must be wondering who we are."

"You're the Company of Merchant Adventurers," Dev said. He caught Lot's shocked expression; she had taken the time to read the debriefing notes after the Black Knight incident. Riya, on the other hand, hadn't, so Dev continued as much for her benefit as trying to convince the Suited Man that he knew more than he did.

"You received your charter from Henry IV in 1407 to look for new opportunities, new ways to keep the British Empire's coffers full. You dealt with emerging technology, like Black Knight, but as the Empire fell, you kept a very low profile."

The man nodded pleasantly. "I am impressed you know."

"A friend of mine was caught up working with your bunch. Stephan Ebert."

Riya recognized the name from their past conversations. "You mean Tyker?"

Dev nodded and watched the man's expression carefully. For a moment he looked genuinely upset, before his expression returned to its usual amiable state.

"Yes. In 1897, I believe, the Company recruited him because of his research on solar activity. He was from

Prussia, as I recall." The man shook his head. "And I know about his unfortunate death today at the hands of Winter Storm." He sighed almost theatrically. "But he had a heck of an innings, eh?"

"You know who we are." It was a statement, not a question, and Dev was pleased to see the man didn't know how to handle Dev's confidence. Not that he felt confident inside. There, he felt a seething rage.

"Of course I know who you all are. My name is Fabian Hobson, the Company's chancellor. We have been keeping tabs on the Inventory ever since it was created, and, when the Black Knight incident occurred, we could no longer keep under the radar, so to speak."

Lot was still eating a sandwich, but her curiosity was killing her. "What do you want from us? We haven't got anything left."

"My dear girl, I know you haven't got two sausages to rub together, and that is what bothers us." He slowly paced the room, his finger dancing like a conductor's baton as he spoke. "The World Consortium runs the Inventory, and of course, we have been rivals for . . . well, ever. But, until recently, I would like to think, good-natured rivals. Shadow Helix, however . . . well, that was a different beast."

He stopped and gazed out of the window. Only the sound of the clock shaving time, and the crunch of Riya turning her attention to a plate of cookies, could be heard. Eventually he continued.

"Under the recent reign of Double Helix, Shadow Helix's plans had always revolved around covert ways of taking over the world. Breaking into the Inventory ... and their last scam you were involved with. All that business with the blasted gravity gun. Double Helix was always sneaky. You see, he knew all-out war simply wouldn't work. Subtlety is the key. However, his methods were primitive. So, when he died, Shadow Helix was left a dysfunctional organization. More dysfunctional than normal, that is," he added with a hoarse laugh.

"And you recruited Lee to get Black Knight so the Company could take Helix's place. You know that doesn't make you the good guys, right?" said Dev, standing. He had too much pent-up anger to stay seated any longer. "You're just another secret organization who thinks they should be controlling the world. You're no better than Shadow Helix!"

Fabian moved from the window and smiled. "You know, nobody ever said the World Consortium were the 'good guys' either." He crooked his fingers into air quotes for emphasis. "I mean, look at what your uncle did to you. Look at Kardach, or the Collector." He exhaled his breath in a low "ooohh" to emphasize how bad they were. "Your uncle created monsters, Devon. Now one of those monsters not only has the remains of Shadow Helix behind him, he also has the Inventory. And the only thing stopping him —" he gestured around the room "— is the Company of Merchant Adventurers."

Riya burped loudly as she drank an entire bottle of Coke in one long go. "But you're forgetting, *Fabes ...*"

Fabian grimaced. Riya put her good arm around Dev's shoulders.

"... this boy here is Iron Fist. Without him, they can't get anything out of the Inventory. Without him, the security kicks in and keeps everything locked down there nice and safe. It *don't matter* what the Collector does down there. He's trapped. He's a prisoner."

Fabian smiled, and his eyes met Dev's. "Is she right?"

Dev tensed. He, Tyker and Lot hadn't told anybody about what they had found in the Black Zone. He wasn't even sure if the Collector was aware of the hidden zone, but if he was...

Riya's arm slipped from Dev when he didn't answer. She frowned. "I am right . . . right?"

Lot moved to Dev's side and put her arm over his shoulder, fixing Riya with a look that Dev couldn't help but notice was a little frosty.

"Sorry, Riya, but there's a lot you don't know, since you're new to the team. . . Tell her, Dev."

"Yes, Devon, tell her," said Fabian, studying him carefully.

Dev really didn't want to, but Lot nudged him and nodded. He didn't have a choice.

"There is another zone inside the Inventory. The Black Zone." He saw Riya's frown deepen. He looked at Fabian. "What do you know about it?"

"We know what's in there. That's where, amongst other things of immense value, they kept Ebert, or your Mr Tyker, as he insisted on calling himself. Poor man, woken in the future, his country no longer existing. . . The world changes. Countries come and go. Empires rise and fall . . . and secrets are kept." Fabian's eyes gleamed with intrigue as he flashed a glance between Dev and Riya.

Dev sighed. "You know I have this synaesthesia power." Riya gave a single nod, waiting for him to continue. "It was created; I was created — like the

Collector." He hung his head. He only continued when Lot reassuringly squeezed his hand.

"But we found out something else. Me, Lot and Tyker. Hidden in the Black Zone is a storage facility. It's full of clones." He took a deep breath. "It's full of other versions of . . . *me*."

Riya couldn't find her words, so blinked in surprise. Fabian continued on Dev's behalf.

"All empty shells, of course. The real Dev, the person you know, is in his head. The convenient thing is that he can be extracted and popped into a fresh new body when this one —" he waved a hand at Dev "— is about to die. We call it the Eternal Machine."

Riya slumped into the chair Dev had vacated. "So how many times have you died?"

Dev shrugged. "Maybe once. Maybe ten times. Maybe never."

Fabian picked up a sandwich and checked its filling. "Why do they have to put cucumber on everything?" He removed the offending slice of vegetable and took a bite. "But that puts us in an interesting position. The Collector now has more than one Devon, more than one Iron Fist with which he can unlock security and take what he wants from the Inventory."

Riya nodded in understanding. "In other words, he has the keys to the castle?"

"*If* he knows about the Black Zone," said Dev. "And *if* he can find it."

"It won't take him long if he doesn't know already," muttered Lot gloomily. "Then, like you said, he has the whole of Shadow Helix and the Inventory at his disposal." She noticed Fabian was smiling. "I don't see what's so funny about that?"

"Because you don't see what I see. The Collector may have all these Devon clones. He has the hardware, but he doesn't have –" he tapped Dev on the head "– the software."

"You mean he needs my consciousness?"

"Indeed. Which is why he sent Winter Storm after you."

"But Winter Storm tried to kill my uncle first. . ."

Fabian nodded. "Yes. I suspect that is because your uncle must have a bigger secret still left to tell. And we at the Company would also very dearly like to know what it is."

Dev's eyes narrowed. "Do you have an idea?"

Fabian raised his eyebrows. "Let us just pray that he recovers quickly so we can ask. . ."

LIVING THE DREAM

Fabian Hobson left them alone again. This time Lot was the only one who tried the door and windows, just in case they had been unlocked.

"It's a prison, Lot," said Dev with a sigh. He tapped the oak-panelled walls. "We can't kick our way out of this. The glass is probably bulletproof, and there is nothing for my synaesthesia to work with."

Lot slumped on to the end of a chaise longue in the corner. For the first time in a long while, she looked defeated. Dev was surprised to find that this alarmed him more than his uncle being critically ill, Wade missing,

Tyker dead, Winter Storm wanting to suck out his brain and the Collector seizing the Inventory with his friends trapped inside.

It had been a pretty awful twenty-four hours.

Lot's constant good nature, infectious smile and bright outlook had carried him through dark times before, and he couldn't bear losing her. But he couldn't bring himself to tell her how he felt.

He was glad when Riya broke the silence.

"Why keep us prisoner if we're on the same side?"

"We're not on the same side," said Lot quietly. "We just have a mutual enemy."

Riya shrugged. "The enemy of my enemy is my friend." They both looked at her. "It's from a film or something." She lapsed into a thoughtful silence for a little longer, then: "So if the Collector gets this Eternal Machine..."

"He can live for ever," Dev finished. The Collector's plan was genius in its sheer simplicity. World domination, committing increasingly elaborate crimes – it was all fine for a villain who knew he had limited time on the planet. But to be able to live for ever – the Collector would have the ultimate prize.

Riya thought about it. Then, as pragmatic as ever, she

threw up her hands. "Well, it seems to me the answer is simple."

"We stop him?" said Lot, her voice laced with sarcasm.

"We destroy the Inventory." There was no trace of irony in Riya's voice. She absolutely meant it.

The room door clicked open again and Fabian entered. A doctor followed, pushing a wheelchair that was bedecked with computers, screens and monitoring equipment that was connected to Charles Parker, who sat in the midst of it all, wearing a plain green dressing gown. His eyes were closed, his face covered in sensors, and he wore a skullcap that had an assortment of wires coming from it. Dev noticed his bare arms and legs were bound by metal restraints attached to the chair. He also caught Fabian's knowing look as he closed the door behind them.

"The electronics are all self-contained and don't lead anywhere outside this room, Devon, so please don't go getting any ideas about trying to sabotage the whole system."

"What have you done to him?"

"He's in a medically induced coma." Fabian held up his hand to stop Dev from overreacting. "And he's fine.

Or at least, he's in a much better state than he was when I brought him here. I must say, your quick thinking taking him to the hospital may have saved his life. We have done our best here to mend bones and internal injuries. The Company's medical facilities are *almost* as good as yours. Except we can't bring people back from the dead."

Dev scowled, but didn't say anything.

Riya raised her plaster cast. "Hey, then maybe sort this thing out."

"In good time," Fabian said dismissively.

The doctor positioned the wheelchair in the centre of the room while Fabian lowered blinds across the windows, creating pools of shadows around them.

"However, I must warn you that his injuries were so severe that he is not out of the woods yet. His condition is still critical. That also means we must talk with him as quickly as possible."

"And how do you propose we do that?" asked Lot, walking over to Charles's side and combing a lock of grey hair from his eyes.

Fabian wagged a finger. "That is a very good question, my young lady."

"I am not your lady," Lot snapped. Dev was pleased to see Fabian hesitate; he hadn't expected to be answered back. "And we can't think of a single reason we should be helping the Company. You said you want information from him. That's not the same as helping."

Fabian quickly composed himself. "We have no desire to see the Collector live for ever, especially while wielding the combined power of Shadow Helix and the Inventory. That is a battle we will lose. One *the world* will lose. Like it or not, you and I are working together. And it doesn't stop with finding out what Parker knows." He nodded towards Dev. "Your gift will be needed more than ever. There is nobody at the Company who can do what you do. We have ethical lines we dared not cross by manipulating humans. He —" another nod to Charles in the chair, who had just started to drool "— had no such qualms. Remember that next time you accuse us of being the baddies."

Dev sighed. "OK, we'll help. But we'll only do it with Sergeant Wade."

Fabian's expression softened. "Nobody can contact your good sergeant. The World Consortium is in chaos and she . . . she is presumed dead. I'm sorry."

He looked genuinely sorry too. Dev was surprised when the ordinarily stoic Riya couldn't hold back a loud sob. Wade had recruited her from the Brazilian slums and given her a remarkable opportunity to work at the Inventory. The opportunity had changed her life, and she couldn't thank Wade enough. Dev gave Lot a hug and felt a shudder of sorrow course through her. She looked up at Dev with glassy eyes.

"Too many people have suffered, Dev. We've got to stop him, no matter the cost."

Dev nodded and reluctantly let her go. He regarded his uncle and sucked in a deep breath to calm his nerves. "How can we talk to him?"

"The TelePath artefact you had." He laughed at Dev's surprised expression. "Oh, we know plenty about what goes on inside the Inventory," he said with a deliberate sense of mystery before waving his hand to dismiss the revelation. "Anyway, it allows the channelling of thoughts and memories. *This* contraption –" he circled a finger around the skullcap on Charles's head "– performs a similar function, except rather than store memories, it allows us to plug straight into the human brain. With this, we can peer into people's *dreams*."

Despite the torrent of bad news, Lot's interest was piqued. "You can watch people's dreams?"

Fabian smiled. "Oh yes. You see, the brain is like Mr Winter's bio-bots. An organic network of living tissue.

That's why your synaesthesia doesn't work on them. Except, it theoretically could."

Dev was puzzled. "My power only works on electronics."

Fabian bit his upper lip as he considered how to phrase his point. "Yes . . . and no. It works on electronics and electricity. You can't affect the living because there is no interface into their brains. Technically, if you could get inside here —" he tapped the side of his own head "— you could surf away. . ."

He let that idea settle in.

Dev ran a hand along the cables leading from Charles Parker's skullcap. "So if I use my power on these wires, I can get into his head. . ."

Fabian crossed to his side, unable to hide the excitement in his voice. "You would be inside this machine, able to see and experience his dreams. But we can only watch." He grabbed Dev's hand and held it in front of his face. "You have the power to communicate. To interact."

"What's the catch?" Everybody looked at Riya, who was wiping her bloodshot eyes. "There's got to be a catch, right?"

"The catch is that it has never been attempted before. It may not work. It may go wrong and Dev's mind will be trapped inside Parker's. . . There are many ways it can go wrong." Fabian put his hand on Dev's shoulder. "But if you don't try, the Collector will already have won."

Dev looked at Lot and saw her nod encouragement.

"I'll do it. What is it you want me to ask?"

"Ask him, 'Where is it?'"

"Where's what?"

"Ah, that's another problem. In dream states we are all susceptible to outside influence. For example, if Riya here was asleep and we put her hand in a cup of water, she may very well dream of being in the sea, drowning, or dream of weeing herself, which she would then do in the real world."

"Try it and you're history," she growled.

"If you ask him a specific question in a dream, such as 'Where is the whale?', his subconscious, his dream, could simply make up any answer and it will believe the whale is real. Which is useless."

Lot understood. "So Dev will be tricking him into revealing the answer?"

"Correct, young ... Lottie. And due to the current situation, I assure you what we need to know will be in the front of his mind." He placed the cable firmly into Dev's hand. "Ask, and you shall receive."

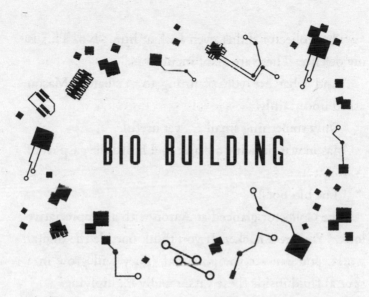

BIO BUILDING

Shelving units the size of office blocks had been moved aside for the four huge steel vats that now stood in the middle of the Green Zone. The vats themselves were as big as houses, with vertical windows from top to bottom so technicians could see the contents.

Mason and Aaron watched helplessly as a dozen huge 3D printers quickly churned out an array of machine parts. An army of technicians put them together to form a new machine that was connected to the vats.

"This is your grand plan?" Mason asked as mockingly as he dared.

The Collector didn't even look at him. "No. This is my defence. These are giant incubators."

"And what are you planning to ... bate?" Mason asked uncertainly.

"Only something small ... yet useful."

Mason was drawing a blank, but heard the gasp from Aaron.

"The bio-bots!"

The Collector glanced at Aaron with an appreciative look. "You are a hacker. If you think outside the digital world, you can see the potential. They will grow in a special fluid inside these vats, rapidly multiplying."

"Sorry, what am I missing?" said Mason, looking between Aaron and the Collector.

"How many bio-bots are there?" Aaron asked, awed.

"There must be hundreds..." Maths was never Mason's strongest subject.

"Trillions," the Collector said. "All working together. Onslow Winter foresaw millions of his bio-bots working together on construction sites. He didn't see the bigger picture. Imagine a swarm of trillions, all at my control. All created right here."

"Like I said, Onslow Winter is a genius," said Aaron. Despite his opinion of Winter crashing to an all-time low, he still clung to the hope he had misinterpreted Winter's previous cowardly act. "He would've put something in them, some kind of self-destruct, just so maniacal villains like yourself couldn't do this."

The Collector slowly turned to face Aaron and drew himself to his full height. "Maniacal? Me? This is a plan I instigated when I worked with Double Helix on his plan for the synchro-cogitron. I saw he was just out for petty power grabs, to control weak minds. I saw a day I would take over Shadow Helix. I saw a day I would crush Charles Parker. Do you think for a moment I have left any of this to chance? That I would allow Winter to weaken his greatest creation?"

Aaron wasn't backing down. "He is smarter than you."

"Why don't you ask him yourself?"

Aaron and Mason spun around. Onslow Winter was walking towards them. The confident stride they remembered from his office had been replaced with a slight limp, his left foot dragging on the ground.

"You're alive!" cried Aaron with relief. He was about to say something more, when he noticed the skin across Winter's face ripple as if pushed by something beneath. Moments later his lame foot corrected itself and he was walking normally. "He's infected, isn't he? Another of your remote-controlled puppets?"

The Collector nodded. "Like the security guard you met, yes. Remote-controlled people are such fun. Who should we infect next? The leader of a great superpower, perhaps? I could instruct him to place his twitching finger on the button to launch a nuclear missile. Wouldn't that be fun?"

"Except I'm not a puppet," said Onslow Winter with a smile.

Aaron and Mason exchanged puzzled looks.

The Collector barked with delight. "Oh, you poor fools. You don't understand, do you? You see, the bio-bots were stolen from the Red Zone by me. Charles Parker had no idea of their true potential. And if truth be known, neither did I. I needed a willing subject to experiment on."

Winter proudly patted his chest. "And here I am. You see, I was dying. My disease was terminal. They had no cure because they didn't even have a name for it." He gestured towards the Collector. "Then along he comes and offers to cure me with the bio-bots if I used my formidable intellect to develop them into the ultimate weapon. Better still, when he told me about his plan to get back in here... Imagine my delight at the thought of getting revenge on the very people who took my greatest invention from me."

Aaron suddenly understood. "Eema's biochip."

"*My* biochip," Winter snapped back. "The one that would have revolutionized my company! The bio-bots replace the disease, they become part of me. I get cured and have my revenge in one stroke."

The Collector suddenly grabbed both Aaron and Mason behind their necks. His grip was so strong that they couldn't help dropping to their knees. Onslow Winter stopped in front of them and extended his hand. Each finger turned grey and elongated in a stream of bio-bots that extended towards the boys. They heard the Collector's low voice close to their ears.

"I could infect you both right now and you couldn't resist." The bio-bot tentacles stopped centimetres from their faces. "I would rather not, but I do require some information from you."

Mason licked his dry lips. "W-What information? You already have everything."

"Almost. But there is something in here that is hidden from us all, and I know Dev and Lot found out about it."

The boys exchanged a worried look.

"H-He might have said something," Mason said quickly, "but to be honest, when Dev goes on, I tend to tune out and start daydreaming."

The tentacles edged closer towards them. So close, Mason was almost cross-eyed trying to focus on them dancing in front of his eyes.

"I hope for your sake you are wrong," whispered the Collector. "Now, tell me where I will find the entrance to the Black Zone."

Aaron and Mason exchanged another look, wondering if the name meant anything to the other. Mason felt sick; he had never heard Dev mention it, and now it looked as if that was another of his friend's secrets that was going to get him killed.

DREAM COME TRUE

Dev knew it was ironic to say it was just like falling asleep, but the moment he allowed his synaesthesia to flow into the cables attached to his uncle's skullcap and he followed the flow of the current into the man's brain, it felt as if he had stepped through that foggy barrier between wakefulness and sleep.

Normally his synaesthesia felt like an extension of his senses. He could explore a computer system in his mind's eye, while still being aware of what was happening around him in the physical world. But this was different. As he entered Charles Parker's dream, his synaesthesia seemed to melt away and Dev found himself standing in darkness, although he could see himself perfectly, even if there was no obvious source of light.

Then a landscape emerged around him, formed from countless pixels of light. As far as Dev could tell it was a rolling field; an oak towered over him, shielding him from the sun. The landscape shimmered like a mirage, the details blurred. Dev reached out and was surprised to find he could feel the tree bark under his fingers.

"Weird," he said in a low voice.

Fabian's voice boomed across the landscape. "You're part of his dream. His mind is tricking you into thinking the tree is real."

Dev looked around, expecting Fabian to step from behind the tree. "Where are you?"

"Still in the Company House, observing you. I can talk directly to you, but I won't be able to intervene. Be careful, Devon."

"Careful? Of what?"

Before Fabian could answer, a pair of shapes emerged from the haze. Dev found it disturbing to look at them, their faces switched from being blank to having basic features — eyes, nose, mouth — that lacked any detail. He was reminded of the obscured faces lying in the cryopods beneath a sheen of condensation.

He had the impression that one was Charles Parker, looking many years younger. The other was a woman of possibly the same age whose face teetered on the edge of recognition – had he seen her before?

They were talking, laughing and holding hands. The image glitched, like a badly tuned TV signal, and the next moment the woman was suddenly on a crude swing hanging from the oak tree, being pushed by Charles. They were much closer to Dev, but still didn't pay him any attention.

"Can they see me?" Dev whispered.

Charles Parker looked straight at Dev. "Yes," he said, then turned back to the woman and continued laughing as if nothing had happened.

Dev felt as if he shouldn't be here. Dev had had Tyker inside his head, but it felt wrong to be inside somebody else's head. He stepped forward and spoke as clearly as he could.

"Where is it?"

The woman stopped swinging so abruptly, Dev was surprised she didn't fall off. The next moment she was standing in front of him, looming down like a giant. Her face was still distorted, as if trapped behind opaque glass. It took a moment for Dev to understand he was looking up at her from the point of view of a small child.

"What's happening?"

"You're in his dream. His rules." Fabian's voice didn't seem to be audible to the other two.

The woman cocked her head quizzically. "This is *him*?"

Dev felt uneasy. He stepped around the woman so he could address Charles Parker again. "Where is it?"

Charles frowned. "Where is *what*?"

"I don't know," Dev blurted. He flinched as the woman bent over, reached out and touched his face. Her hand felt warm and he was surprised to smell a familiar strong floral scent. "I just want to know where it is."

Charles tilted his head back and gave out a long "aaaahh" of comprehension. "You mean the second one?"

Dev blinked in surprised. Before he could further, the woman stood back upright.

"He's exactly like how I thought my son would look!"

Lot jumped in surprise when Dev's whole body convulsed and he dropped to his knees without letting go of the cable. She reached out for him, but Fabian gently stopped her.

"I wouldn't take that chance," he warned.

"What's happened to him?"

"People's minds may be lots of electrical signals running hither and thither, but Dev is also experiencing Parker's emotions as a side effect. If you suddenly pull him out of it, who knows what will happen? Like waking a sleepwalker."

"What happens if you wake a sleepwalker?" Riya asked curiously.

"They die."

"Sounds like a tall tale to me."

Fabian gestured to Dev. "Do you care to risk it?"

Riya and Lot exchanged a worried look, but Lot slowly moved her hand away and turned her attention to one of the screens on the wheelchair. It was playing the dream from Charles Parker's point of view, with Dev and the woman appearing as wispy, ill-defined shapes. Even as she watched, the dreamscape was twirling as if they were standing inside a tornado and re-forming into something that resembled a corridor in the Inventory.

Dev reached for the woman, but she vanished before his eyes. One moment she was there, the next she was indistinguishable from the corridor wall, with Charles Parker walking ahead.

Charles turned as he walked. He was still an ill-defined photofit, but was back to his current age. "Hurry up, Devon, or we'll miss it."

"Miss what?" said Dev, surprised to find he was out of breath trying to catch up. No matter how fast he was, his uncle's casual strides were able to keep him further ahead. "Wait! Slow down!" With the bizarre logic of dreams, Dev was now running flat out while his uncle stayed ahead, walking normally. "And where is she?"

"Where is who?"

"That woman. Sh-She was my mother?"

"Almost there," said Charles, ignoring the question.

They passed through a door and into an unfamiliar circular room. The door was angled into the floor and sloped up into the centre of the dome-shaped room. Panoramic windows offered a view of only darkness beyond, while control panels vaguely reminded Dev of the Inventory's control bunker.

"Hello, three-oh-two point two!"

Dev whirled around to see Eema bounce towards them. Actually bounce, like a giant spacehopper. Her cheery yellow holograph head beamed at him.

"I'm Dev..." He felt disoriented as Eema came

to a stop next to Charles, who was busy typing on a computer. "This is just a dream," he reminded himself under his breath.

Fabian's voice resonated around the room. "You're doing well, Devon. Find out where you are."

Dev walked around the computer, glancing at the screen for any clues. Whatever Charles was typing on the computer appeared as a mess of splodges and shapes. The view outside gave no hints. Dev suspected the moment he got their location from Charles, Fabian would pull him from the dream — and right now he had more burning questions. He leaned over the computer terminal, getting in Charles Parker's oddly blurred face as best he could.

"I saw my mother. Who is she?"

Charles reacted with surprise. "She's your mother, Devon. Of sorts. People like you don't have real mothers."

Dev slammed his fists on the computer monitor. The casing cracked and the screen shattered. Evidently in the dream world he had super strength. "Who is she?!"

Charles's placid expression turned to anger. The light in the room seemed to dim, and Dev felt the atmosphere around him change. It felt unwelcoming.

"Devon," said Fabian. "I don't think you should aggravate him. His vital signs here are beginning to peak. Don't forget, he's still critically ill and you are an uninvited guest in his head."

"I don't care!" roared Dev. He was sick of the lies woven around him. Guilty about the people they had lost in keeping secrets, and the fact it took voices in his head or other people's dreams to reveal the truth. "I want answers. Who is she?"

Charles slowly drew himself to his full height, and once again Dev found himself looking up from a much smaller perspective. His uncle was almost twice as tall as he was, and his voice was suddenly deep and threatening.

"She went away because of you!"

"Who is she?" He saw Charles's hands bunch into fists. "You can't hurt me. This is just a dream."

Charles Parker's voice dropped to a hiss. "Oh, is it?"

Dream or not, Dev felt Charles's fist like a sledgehammer to his chest. He soared across the room, smashing through three control panels in a shower of sparks before he slid to a halt. The pain he was experiencing felt very real indeed. He tried to stand, but Eema bounded over, knocking him back to the floor.

With a roar of fury, Dev placed his hands against Eema and tried to summon his synaesthesia to fry her circuits. Nothing happened. He looked at his hands in surprise.

"This is Parker's dream, not yours," said Fabian's omnipresent voice.

Dev was suddenly yanked off his feet by his gigantic uncle, who held him by his throat. Dev fought for breath, and no amount of telling himself it was only a dream would stop the sensation of choking.

Charles pulled Dev so closed they were nose-to-nose, his face transforming between his own, the Collector's and Kardach's – the Shadow Helix henchman who his uncle had also created in a lab.

"I lost her because of you!" Charles snarled. "And you wonder why I hated you so much?"

In shock, Dev stopped struggling. He had always regarded Charles as his uncle. That's what he called himself. Even when he discovered Charles had created the Collector, Kardach and himself, he couldn't quite call Charles Parker his *father*. That was a term the Collector had mockingly used. But now, seeing his mother, he knew there was no escaping that fact.

"Dad. . ." Dev began.

Fabian's voice echoed through the room. "Now you've done it. . ."

Rage twisted Charles Parker's face and he lifted Dev higher, squeezing the breath from him.

"You want to know her name?" he roared – then he threw Dev across the room. "It's——"

The explosion of glass around Dev drowned out the words as he was propelled through the window like a cannonball.

He rolled to the ground outside, kicking up a cloud of fine grey dust. Dev reached for his throat, wondering why he still couldn't breathe. He could see Charles Parker clambering through the broken window to chase him. Dev struggled to his feet and noticed the landscape around him. Jagged grey hills were set against a bejewelled black sky, and high above——

The white, blue, brown marble known as Earth. Washed on the moon? No, he couldn't be. Further beyond was the moon.

Dev dropped back to his knees as he began choking to death in the hostile vacuum of space.

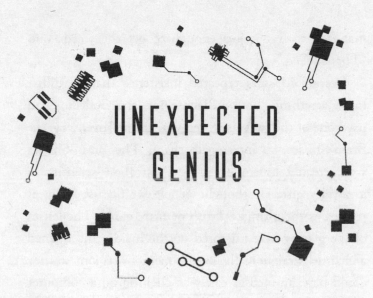

UNEXPECTED GENIUS

Norman the technician removed the mirrored shades that Mason had been forced to wear. It took several moments for his eyes to adjust to the bright lights of the medical bay, but when they did, he could see Norman speaking to the Collector close to the room's only door. Norman couldn't help but cast apologetic glances; Mason knew if the technician had refused to help, the Collector would have killed him on the spot.

Mason's neck was sore as he turned his head to see Aaron sitting on a bed opposite him, staring with wide eyes. Mason tried to speak, but his mouth was dry. He managed to wet it just enough to get the words out. "That sucked."

Despite Mason's repeated insistence that he didn't know anything about a Black Zone, the Collector had used one of the gadgets stored within the Inventory, the Brain-Shades, to interrogate them. The Brain-Shades were created by an eccentric Australian scientist as a novelty gift. He thought people would use them at parties as the ultimate Truth or Dare game. The lenses of the glasses were mirrored on the inside, and opened a channel straight to the brain's memory regions so they could be examined as easily as clicking on a computer file. Unfortunately, the side effect was that they often rendered the wearer insane.

Aaron was still staring at him with wide eyes.

"What're you staring at?"

"Your hair's gone white," Aaron said.

Like Aaron, Mason was cuffed to the metal rail at the side of the bed, but he could sit up enough to see his reflection in a mirror. Sure enough, his head of tangled hair was now snow white. Somehow that upset him even more than having his brain tortured.

The Collector spoke up, drawing both their attention.

"It seems your friend didn't trust you with secrets

after all. We are going to have to perform the search the old-fashioned way and tear this place apart a section at a time. It also means I have little use for you both. You're expendable."

He turned away and left the room with Norman, closing the door behind them. Mason dropped back on the bed, feeling utterly exhausted.

"How long was I out?"

"About an hour? I heard him receive a call. He . . . he said the Winter Storm incubators are operational."

"And now he'll be making billions of bio-bots thanks to your hero, Onslow."

"That's not fair," Aaron said, pulling at his handcuffs for the hundredth time. "How was I supposed to know he was only interested in saving his own skin? That whole Winter Storm press conference, the Collector stealing it all and that SonicBoom . . . it was just a show to get our attention."

Mason sat up so suddenly the room spun around him. He caught his balance. "Well, it worked."

"They controlled Chief Hammer at Winter House to lure us in. Separate and destroy the team one by one. . ."

Events from the last day or so danced through Mason's mind. "They make us leave the Inventory —

Charles Parker, Wade, us — knowing it would be left under Eema's control while we handle the crisis . . . except there is no crisis. It's all staged. That's why Winter had that amber shield thing. It was the only way to get him inside here. . ."

Now Aaron was buying into the plan. "With the bio-bots smuggled inside him, Eema's sensors didn't detect them through the amber casing—"

"And once he was freed, wallop!" Mason slapped his thigh for emphasis. "They're loose inside the Inventory."

Aaron shook his head as everything became obvious. "Of course, they easily infected Eema because Winter made the biochip inside her. That brought her under the Collector's control. She just opened the door and let him walk right in."

Mason nodded. "And now he controls her, he has access to everything, but he still can't bypass the Iron Fist security. He can't get them out without Dev."

"Great. So he'll stay here, and we're stuck with him."

"He's not trapped, he could just leave without any tech. . . So whatever is in this Black Zone must be something really special. More special than the contents of the entire Red Zone."

Now Aaron was thinking hard, trying to recall every

word the Collector had uttered. "He said he was creating more bio-bots for defence. I bet that means Dev and the others are still out there and he knows they're going to try and break in."

"We can't just sit here and let him build another army of bios."

Aaron raised his arm and indicated to the cuffs. "We don't have a choice."

Mason laughed and shuffled off the bed. "You know, Charles Parker once told me that out of all the items stored here, there was only one truly great invention."

"A laser gun? That would be useful right about now."

"No. The wheel."

Mason kicked the brake pedal locking the bed's wheels. He sniggered at the look on Aaron's face as he realized that these hospital beds, just like in all other hospitals, were on wheels. Mason pushed his bed across the room so he could reach a set of drawers holding various medical implements.

"Parker is always full of nuggets of advice. He's old school. He prefers the simplest of inventions. Always said they were almost foolproof. Like this one."

Mason pulled a bone saw from the drawer. Its smooth chrome finish sparkled under the lights. "I've been in this medical bay enough times to see what they keep in here. Something for every emergency." He began to quickly hack through the cuff's chain.

Aaron was impressed. "Mase, take this as a one-time-only compliment that I will never, ever repeat to the others. But sometimes, you can be a genius."

DOUBLE
TROUBLE

Dev jolted awake and spluttered to catch his breath. He was sitting in the armchair back in the Company's house. Lot and Riya watched him with concern. Fabian leaned over him with a glass in his hand, the contents of which he had just poured down Dev's throat, which now burned.

"What was that?" he said, wheezing.

Fabian looked at the glass, and placed it back next to a crystal decanter filled with amber liquid. "Our finest brandy. It will put hairs on your chest."

Dev coughed. "I don't want a hairy chest."

"Well, at least it brought you around. I told you not to provoke your uncle inside his own head."

Dev looked around. There was no sign of Charles Parker. "Where is he?"

Fabian looked at Lot to deliver the news. Her brow creased with a frown.

"The emotional strain he went through pushed him deeper into his coma. They had to rush him to a life-support machine." He held up a hand to assure Dev. "He's fine now. Well, stable. I promise you, he is more than likely going to be fine." He watched Dev's reaction carefully. "Tell me what you saw."

Dev shook his head. "It was a dream. You can't guarantee any of that was real. What do you know about my mother?"

Fabian smiled sadly. "Devon, you are the Inventory's top-secret project. We know very little about you. If the Company intended to be hostile towards you, we would have scanned the minds of your two friends here and quickly learned everything they know. However, from Charles Parker's brain scan I can tell you everything you saw came from the limbic system, which is key in processing memories. We're sure he wasn't making things up, no matter how strange they may have seemed to you."

"Did you recognize the woman . . . your mother?" Lot asked softly.

Fabian waved his hand in irritation. "I'm sorry, but that is far from the pressing point right now. Time is very much against us. Can you confirm where your uncle took you?"

Dev replayed the events in his mind and shivered at the frightening memory of his uncle going berserk. "I don't understand where I actually was. I mean, what are we looking for? You can tell me now, right?"

All eyes turned to Fabian. He walked to the window and gazed at Tower Bridge. "The Company has always focused on exploring where technology could take us, developing more, gathering the best ideas and latest advances. The World Consortium, on the other hand, was most concerned about keeping it out of the public's hands. That's why they created the Inventory." He moved both hands up and down like a scale. "The balance was kept between us. A friendly competition that didn't have the need to resort to violence. Then Shadow Helix came along and upset that."

"We've kinda figured all that out by now," said Riya impatiently.

"The Inventory was suddenly under threat. They created ingenious security." He glanced fleetingly at Dev. "But that wasn't enough. Tell me, with your computers, your phones, what do you do to preserve your data?"

"We back them up," said Lot. "Redundancies." Then her eyes widened the same time Dev's did.

Only Riya looked around, puzzled. "Redundancies?"

"It's a backup site!" Dev yelped. "They built a second Inventory!"

Fabian turned from the window and extended his arms like a showman. "Bingo! Why build one when you can have two?" He eagerly crossed to Dev and knelt by his side. "We knew they'd built it in an inaccessible location, one that is completely automated, so no staff come in or out. The images from the dream were too hazy to be sure, but now we have a likely candidate. I just need you to confirm our suspicions."

"What's to stop the Company looting it?" said Dev.

"Nothing. Nothing except our honour. But you should know that inside the backup site are the tools you will require if you have any hope of stopping the Collector." Fabian offered his hand for Dev to shake. "We need each other."

Dev reluctantly shook his hand. Fabian beamed with delight. "So, where is it?"

"I was in orbit. I could see the Earth, so I thought I might have been on the moon. The land had mountains, it was grey . . . but I could also see the moon, up in the sky. It doesn't make sense."

Fabian hopped from one foot to the other in a delighted jig. "Aha! Of course! Waltemath's moon!" He noticed their blank expressions. "Most people think the Earth has only one moon, which is nonsense of course. In 1898 a Hungarian scientist announced his discovery of a tiny moon, all based purely on calculations. He named it Lilith. Of course, nobody believed him because they couldn't see it. Its orbit kept it in perpetual daylight from Earth's point of view, so it couldn't be seen in blue sky."

"We have more than one moon?" Lot echoed, surprised by the news.

"Of course! Don't you ever look on the internet?" He shook his head in bewilderment. "The kids of today. Lazy. Lilith is the ideal place for a backup Inventory!" Fabian declared.

Riya pulled a face. "And that helps us how? The moon . . . a moon? I mean, come on! It was bad enough Dev managed to get to Black Knight and that was just in orbit overhead. The moon's . . . a little bit further."

"A bit, yes," Fabian said smoothly. "But if you recall, it was the Company who put Black Knight into orbit back in Queen Victoria's reign."

"That device you have." Dev nodded to Fabian's watch. "That teleported us here, right? Can we use that?"

Fabian held up his watch so they could see its face. There was no dial, but a series of small entwined discs with numbers etched on them. "You are correct; it is a teleport device. These are longitude and latitude coordinates. It works with a rather impressive satellite system overhead. That stretching and squashing sensation you felt was most of your atoms passing through them."

Lot frowned at Dev and mouthed the word *Most?* She was wondering what parts of her had been left behind.

Fabian continued. "Which means teleportation remains an earthbound activity." He winked at Lot. "And yes, use it too much and you will start . . . thinning out. And not in a good way."

Lot clicked her fingers. "What about that young tech guy . . . Eryl Stoker! He owes us a favour."

Stoker was an entrepreneur who had built his own private spacecraft exploration company, Space Rangers, from scratch. His Osprey rocket had been stolen by Lee – an ex-associate of the Collector's.

Dev looked sidelong at Fabian. "That's right. In fact, wasn't Lee working for you guys when he stole Stoker's rocket, launched himself into space and tried to kill me?"

"We didn't order him to kill you. And that's water under the bridge. We're all friends now, remember? You shook on it. Besides, his rockets could get us into orbit, but no further. Getting to Waltemath's moon will need a little extra push."

"And your uncle wiped Stoker's memory, so he wouldn't remember who we are," said Riya. "Doesn't the Company have any cool spacecraft?"

"I wish. Back to square one," Fabian sighed.

"Maybe not," said Dev thoughtfully. "There may just be somebody who can help us after all."

GOING OLD SCHOOL

Mason was impressed with the speed at which Aaron tackled the lock on the medical bay door. Using a sharp knife that looked more at home in a kitchen than a hospital, Aaron levered the cover panel off the door's keypad.

"Hacking is not just about the internet, y'know," he said softly as he studied the wires on the panel behind. "The term actually came from people rewiring hardware like this ... so it was able to perform a different task from the one it was designed to do. . ."

"Fascinating," said Mason, glazing nervously at the security camera.

Aaron quickly followed his gaze. The camera was in the centre of the room and didn't need to move, as its lens could see 360 degrees. Aaron had placed a small circular plaster that would only obscure the view of the door but not the rest of the room, so anybody watching the footage would think a spot of dirt was on the lens. Then they sat back and waited. If anybody had been watching them over a security monitor, they would no doubt send somebody to investigate. After twenty minutes they were satisfied that the Collector and his men were all too busy to notice, so they then turned their attention to opening the door.

"Relax. They can't see us." He turned back to the wires and pulled a green one free. He pressed it against an orange wire and the door hissed open. "Boom!" Aaron exclaimed.

They poked their heads into the corridor, which gently curved out of view in both directions. The coast was clear, but Mason knew from past experience that the moment they stepped out, they would be at the mercy of Eema's advanced security system. Last time they had relied on Dev to fool the cameras; this time they were on their own.

Aaron nudged Mason. "Now what?"

Mason heard footsteps coming their way; more than one person. They were close to the canteen, so he hoped it was just some harmless Inventory technicians.

"Now we go old school." Mason reached across for a fire extinguisher in the corner of the room.

The sound of gentle talking grew louder. Mason couldn't quite make out the words, but he heard a low laugh. He tensed for a few more seconds as the voices drew nearer – then he stepped out and fired the extinguisher, first at the feet of the approaching men, then at their faces.

It had the desired effect. The two men wore the Collector's military uniforms, but carried their helmets under their arms as they talked. Mason's first shot spread thick foam across the floor – the second was perfectly aimed, blasting the foul-tasting foam around their feet and into their mouths. The men slipped backwards on the slick foam, falling hard on to their backs. One cracked his head on the floor, knocking himself out. The other scrambled to stand, but Mason clunked him across the head with the empty extinguisher. Now it was Aaron's turn to be impressed.

"We're unstoppable!" he whooped, giving Mason a high-five.

Mason was already dragging one of the guards into the medical bay by his feet.

"Get the other one."

Standing in the camera's blind spot, they took off the men's uniforms, then dragged them to the hospital beds — back in view of the camera — and positioned them with their faces away from the camera, so it looked as if they had fallen asleep. Since no alarms had sounded, they guessed they'd got away with their deception. Mason removed the plaster from the camera, Aaron sparked a pair of wires on the door control so it closed as they hurried through, and they were both on their way in baggy uniforms with helmets covering their faces.

"Now to get out of here," said Aaron as he started down the corridor towards the exit. Mason grabbed his arm to stop him.

"Not yet."

"What? Are you nuts? We can't stay here."

Mason pointed towards the exit. "I guarantee you the Collector will have a small army protecting the way in and out — we will not get through there. Secondly, he is creating more bio-bots for defence. Which means it's going to be harder for Dev and the others to get in here. So we have to sabotage the incubators."

"Oh, right. No problem!" Aaron sighed heavily and then followed Mason down the corridor towards the Green Zone.

As they neared the end of the curving corridor, they saw a uniformed man wielding a laser rifle standing guard at the door to the Green Zone. Aaron faltered, but Mason gave him a gentle nudge in the back.

"Keep walking," Mason hissed. "Just stay cool."

Walking with urgency and purpose, Mason and Aaron marched up to the door. The guard made no attempt to stop them as the door swished open and they entered the Green Zone.

Aaron exhaled heavily; he had been holding his breath without realizing it.

With most of the immediate shelves pushed aside to make room for the incubators, they had a clear view for almost half a kilometre down an expanded aisle. They could see the vats and a knot of people surrounding them. There was smoke rising from the incubators and a dull rumbling sound that grew with intensity as they drew nearer.

"I have a bad feeling about this," Aaron muttered.

As they approached, it became apparent that it was not smoke but a swirling array of bio-bots that flew effortlessly through the air like a swarm of locusts, making the ominous noise that now sounded like a continuous roll of thunder as their numbers increased.

The Collector watched with delight as the flock swelled, making grand sweeping orbits of the space around them. Several technicians monitored the jury-rigged controls wired to the vats, while Eema stood sentinel.

"We're too late," Aaron hissed.

A familiar metallic rumble from overhead drew their attention to the massive hangar doors in the roof that were parting. Normally they allowed aircraft to access the Inventory, but now the collective swarm shot through the doors in a gigantic cloud, bio-bots still joining it as they poured from the incubators.

As the tail of the swarm vanished through the doors, they rolled closed again, filling the hangar with only one sound: the Collector clapping with delight.

"Splendid! Eema, guide the swarm. Let me know when they locate their target."

Mason gently nudged Aaron and whispered, "We've got to destroy that." He nodded towards the vats. "Before he makes any more."

"You two!"

They jumped when they realized the Collector was looking straight at them. Mason knew the criminal's vision allowed him to see through different spectrums of light normal people simply couldn't see. He just hoped he wasn't studying their faces with some thermal or X-ray vision, otherwise their simple disguise would fail.

The Collector marched through his men, uncomfortably close to Mason and Aaron. He crooked his finger. "You two come with me. Time is against us. We must find this Black Zone." He turned on his heel and strode purposefully away. Aaron and Mason reluctantly followed.

Aaron cast one look behind him and could see the incubator vats were already beginning to fill again with bio-bots. For the first time the hopelessness of their situation dawned on him. He prayed that Dev, Lot and Riya were having a better time.

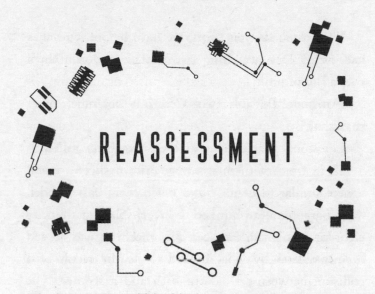

REASSESSMENT

The horizon was filthy black, as if night had come early and blotted out the dividing line between the sky and the rough sea. Fabian stared at it with concern. "It's a cyclone. Once it arrives it will interfere with the link to our teleportation satellites. We shall be stuck here until it passes."

"Good!" said Riya as she bent over, ready to be sick again. The instant teleportation was not agreeing with her.

Fabian undid the top button of his shirt and flapped his tweed jacket to cool down. The air was thick and humid, and he felt as if he was melting alive.

"How long do you think we have before it reaches us?" asked Dev, watching two specks approach them over a hill of junk.

"An hour? Possibly two? Certainly not much more than that."

Lot stood next to Dev as the first object rolled to a halt in front of them — a huge mishmash of a metal sphere similar to Eema, but a much more basic model. A holographic head blinked to life, displaying a blocky eight-bit emoji smiley face. The machine was joined moments later by what looked to be the result of a collision between an old tin bath and a scooter. The vehicle hovered on a cushion of light, and sitting in a reclining chair was an overweight Bangladeshi man wearing a Hawaiian shirt far too small for him. He was the Assessor, and he was grinning from ear to ear, which was a surprise. The last time Dev had seen the Bangladeshi, he'd accidentally demolished the man's house.

"Dev! Lot! Riya! It is so good to see you! What brings you all the way to my empire?"

He gestured behind him, to the rolling hills of junk. It was a massive area of land filled with trash of all kinds — from refrigerators through to entire cargo ships and aircraft. The World Consortium used this area of Bangladesh as their private scrapyard. Everything would be broken down and recycled, whilst any pieces of potentially dangerous technology that filtered through would be sent to the Inventory to be stored.

The Assessor glanced over his shoulder at Fabian, who was desperately fanning himself. "And who's the suit?"

Dev and Lot exchanged a look. Clearly the Assessor hadn't heard the news about the Inventory.

It took a full fifteen minutes for them to explain what had happened. Dev and Lot bounced the story between them with Riya filling in the more gruesome parts. The Assessor listened in silence as they walked – or in the Assessor's case, floated – inland to his home. He threw the occasional glance at Fabian, who kept several paces behind. Only when Dev revealed that the man was with the Company did the Eema unit slow behind Fabian, now acting as a suspicious bodyguard for the Assessor.

They reached the Assessor's home, which looked pretty much as it had before it collapsed – several metal cabins and trailers all welded haphazardly together. The backdrop of junk had changed, and Dev's eyes kept straying to it.

"Is that part of the space elevator?"

A huge metal chain, over a mile long, was coiled behind the house. It was one of the space elevator cables that had saved Dev's life during the Black Knight incident. They had been salvaged from the ocean where they had fallen, and now many small, spherical robots hovered around it like flies. Their mechanical arms were like Swiss army knives, with drills, saws and tiny blowtorches to dismantle it.

The Assessor nodded. "My salvager bots are attempting to recycle it." He looked Fabian up and down. "It appears I have welcomed the enemy into my den."

Fabian gave his best humble smile. "I prefer you think of me as your ally in these dark times." He gestured to the glowering clouds behind them. "Quite literally, in this case. We don't have terribly long."

The Assessor broke into a humourless laugh. "We don't have much time to launch you into space?" He raised his eyebrows at Lot. "You must think I'm a miracle worker."

Lot patted his shoulder. "For the sake of everybody, I really hope you are."

Dev kicked a piece of carbon-fibre panel that blew towards him as the wind picked up. "You have so much here. There has to be something we can use."

"Dev, there doesn't *have to be*," sighed the Assessor. He jerked a thumb at Fabian. "If they couldn't develop a spacecraft, and NASA and Space Rangers can just about do it. . . We're in a junkyard. And you expect me to help save the world with scrap?"

Dev and the Assessor stared at one another for a long moment. Fabian shifted his feet nervously, glancing back at the approaching storm. Dev was the first to crack a smile and look away.

"That's exactly what I think."

The Assessor sighed. "Well, you're a fool." Dev felt his spirits deflate as the Assessor continued. "Although it just so happens that I am a genius. And sometimes it takes a fool to remind a genius that anything is possible. I may have what you need."

The wind scythed over the mounds of junk. It was now an almost constant whistle, increasing with every passing moment. If it wasn't for that, you could have heard a pin drop as everybody looked at the vehicle the Assessor had taken them to see.

Eventually Riya had to ask. "That can fly?"

"It used to be able to. And with a little love and care. . ." The Assessor rolled his head side to side as if to say *maybe*.

"It is a piece of junk," Fabian said flatly.

The Assessor harrumphed. "We *are* in a scrapyard."

"I think it's awesome," said Lot. She hadn't taken her eyes off it. "Where did it come from?"

"Russia," the Assessor said. "They called it the Buran."

It looked like the famous NASA space shuttle. A large, dirty, white aircraft that sat on its belly amongst the junk. A pair of stubby wings still had the faded red letters *CCCP* on the side, the Russian acronym for the USSR. It was smaller than the shuttle by almost twenty metres.

Lot ran her hand along the smooth white fuselage as the Assessor continued:

"It was built in the 1980s by Russia when they were the old Soviet Bloc. It was a rival to the Americans' space shuttle. Officially it made an unmanned launch in 1988. Then the USSR collapsed and they stopped developing it. It was supposed to have been destroyed when its hangar collapsed back in 2002, but truth is we brought it here. In fact, '88 was not its first flight. They had been using this thing for years."

"To do what?" asked Riya.

The Assessor pulled a face, as if the answer was obvious. "Secret government shenanigans, of course."

Dev held up his hand. "OK, but the important questions are: Can we get it launched before the storm hits us? And will it keep us alive once we're up there?"

"Two very good questions," said the Assessor as he typed on a small laptop that formed part of his hover-chair. "Let's see what the salvagers think."

He hit a key. Moments later the swarm of flying robots that had been dismantling the space elevator swooped down and began inspecting the aircraft.

Lot looked down as the floor of compressed junk under her trainers began to vibrate. She thought that it might be an earthquake, but then a battalion of twenty Eema husks appeared, rolling towards them from different points across the scrapyard.

The Assessor smiled at the look on her face. "You didn't think I did all the work around here, did you? I have an army for that!" He laughed, then answered his ringing phone via a headset. The others couldn't make out the words, but his grim face assured them it was bad news. He hung up and stared at the shuttle. "Automated security has detected an inbound object from the west." He indicated the direction in relation to the storm blanketing the southern sky. "It's huge..." He finally looked at the others in turn and took a deep breath. "I think Winter Storm has found us."

THE
BETRAYAL

The mobile X-ray scanner was about the size of a tank and moved on caterpillar tracks. The body was made from six domes, three each side, with the domes pointed towards the wall like reverse satellite dishes. They were connected to a machine in the centre of the chassis. The entire thing was operated by remote control via a mobile phone held by Norman, who looked very sorry for himself as he glanced at the nearest guard's rifle.

"This had originally been developed for search-and-rescue," said the Collector. "The idea had been to locate survivors after earthquakes or landslides by firing a stream of X-rays into the debris, but the intensity of the X-ray pulse tended to kill the very people they were trying to save. Well, it should be perfect for the task at hand, in any case. Begin the scan."

The Collector was standing several metres away as a safety measure, and Mason and Aaron, still doing their best to seem soldierly in their uniform disguises, backed up to a similar distance.

"It's somewhere here, behind these walls," the Collector muttered, almost to himself. "Hidden from view."

A secret within a secret had aroused Mason's curiosity, but the villain was not forthcoming with details.

Norman fiddled with the controls on the phone and the vehicle's engine powered up in near silence. He drove it close to the wall of the warehouse and activated the X-ray domes. A red warning light twirled atop one of the domes, and an alarm on the vehicle quacked a warning. Then an X-ray pulse was fired every second as the vehicle moved at walking pace.

Mason and Aaron could see nothing, but the Collector hissed in pain and looked away, covering his eyes. Only Mason seemed to notice, and remembered the villain's peculiar ability to look through a range of light spectrums. The X-rays may be invisible to everybody else, but to the Collector they were intensely bright flashes.

"Notify me if you find anything," said the Collector, spinning on his heel and walking away.

Mason noticed that they had been left with two of the Collector's troopers and Norman. The odds were evening out ... if only they could think of a plan.

The wind roared and driving rain began to fall in pounding sheets when it struck the rolling hills of junk. The cyclone had turned the entire southern half of the sky black, while the other half was still tropical blue.

The Assessor's fleet of salvager robots had made short work of gently lifting the Buran from the rubbish heap. A tide of finger-sized robots scuttered towards the spacecraft and began to climb over every inch of it, sealing holes and repairing damage. Lot and Riya had helped where they could, while Dev had discussed the overall plan with the Assessor and Fabian.

"That's pretty impressive," Lot had to admit.

Dev glanced from the storm clouds to the west, where the inky cyclone was starting to consume clear blue sky.

"What's happened to Winter Storm? According to the radar it should have been here by now."

The Assessor had been taking regular calls from his automated security centre. "We have had a stroke of luck for once. It seems the cyclone's strong winds are keeping the bio-swarm at bay. If our luck holds, they may not be able to make it."

Dev wasn't sure they had any luck to hold on to, just varying degrees of bad fortune. That was confirmed moments later when the Assessor moved closer to the spacecraft.

"One thing we are lacking is spacesuits," he shouted over the increasing volume of wind and rain. "But as long as you don't leave the shuttle, you won't need them. There will be just enough oxygen on-board the cabin to get you there."

"What about *back*?" said Lot in alarm.

The Assessor swapped a look with Dev, but he didn't answer. Instead, he pointed to the new set of wings that the Eemas were attaching to the shuttle. The wings were three times longer than the shuttle and swept up and backwards. "These are so flexible they could actually wrap around the fuselage, as if cocooning it. Each wing has a grill running along the edge, and a simple hole at the back. They were designed for a special stratospheric glider, built to fly heavy loads. It was believed such gliders would do away with the need for ships crossing the ocean."

"What happened to the glider?" Riya asked suspiciously.

"Oh, you know..." the Assessor mumbled. She was sure she caught the word "crash" in there, but he was already moving on. "The engines are within the wing itself. They don't require fuel. They're a type of eco-ramjet. As you move fast they suck in air and, rather than use that to ignite fuel, it's compressed and pushed out at a higher speed." He indicated enthusiastically at the craft, but faltered when he saw the doubt on the others' faces.

"I don't get it," said Dev. "If the engines don't work until you're moving fast ... how do we start in the first place?"

"Aha!" The Assessor pointed to a construction several metres away. From here it looked like a metal tube that stretched into the distance. They had all seen the salvagers moving to and fro but had assumed they'd been cannibalizing parts to repair the Buran. "We're going to use a catapult!"

Riya couldn't stop herself. "A catapult? This isn't Angry Birds! This is our lives we're talking about!"

"This isn't a giant rubber band. That is an early prototype of a Hyperloop." He waved his hand to silence Dev, who suddenly had a mountain of questions. "It will launch the shuttle at about two hundred miles per hour. Enough to give it lift and allow you to soar into the heart of the cyclone."

Now Lot spoke up. "Wait. What?"

"I was thinking about cats."

Lot blinked in confusion. "Cats?"

The Assessor tapped his temple as he raced to catch up with his thoughts. "They chase birds, and when they do, the birds take off and fly."

"I really don't see—" Dev interjected.

The Assessor waved him into silence with one hand and tapped his head with the other. "Chain of thought! Hush! You see, because the winds inside the storm are about a hundred and twenty miles per hour, a bird couldn't flap its wings. You see?"

Dev, Lot and Riya exchanged confused looks. "No," they answered in chorus.

"Because they'd break. Snap! But they could be like a paper aeroplane instead." He beamed at them as if that explained everything.

"You lost me at cat," said Riya, folding her arms.

"They *glide.*"

"Cats?" said Dev, utterly confused.

The Assessor scowled. "Cats? No. Birds and paper aeroplanes glide. Why are you talking about cats?" Before Dev could answer, he pressed on. "You see, the wind is enough to kick in the ramjets — which alone won't be able to get you in orbit. But they will make you go faster, corkscrewing the shuttle, lifting it very high where there is no air and therefore no air resistance, and it can build up the required speed to break into orbit."

"Which is how fast?" Dev demanded. The last time he had been into orbit he had climbed up the limb of a dangling space elevator.

The Assessor gave a long pause before answering. "Seventeen thousand five hundred miles per hour." The enormous figure hung in the air between them all.

Dev saw Fabian pale. Riya looked apprehensive and his own stomach churned at the thought. But the sight of Lot's eyebrows rising in delight gave him courage; she often saw extreme danger as a chance to have fun.

"What if we——?" Dev began as a faint boom sounded over the wind.

Everybody looked around to see multiple explosions in the sky to the west.

"That's the perimeter defences."

Dev turned to Riya and Lot. "I don't suppose I could convince you two not to come?"

Riya shrugged. "I'd rather do this than go back to the streets of Brazil and end up being controlled by a cloud of tiny robots."

Lot shook her head. "As if you could do it without us."

Dev smiled. "Maybe I could ... but I reckon you're right."

Without warning, Dev lunged and kissed Lot on the lips.

It was his first kiss, and it felt weird and, judging from the movies he had seen, far too sloppy. As he pulled away, her look of shock was replaced with a smile – and they were both burning with embarrassment.

"Now I feel like a third wheel," muttered Riya.

"And, um, I'm so sorry," Dev said to Lot.

Lot's face fell. "For ... the kiss?"

"No." He glanced at Fabian, who suddenly moved in behind Lot and tapped her with the end of his cane. An electric shock pulsed through her and she fell to the ground.

Before Riya realized what had happened, the Assessor

fired a small dart from a tranquillizer gun that had been nestled under his seat. Riya staggered and mumbled incoherently before dropping unconscious.

Dev looked regretfully at Lot and wiped away a tear rolling down his cheek. He looked over at Fabian and gave a curt nod. "Make sure they're safe."

The Assessor waved over a pair of salvager robots which carefully carried them towards the house.

"Good luck, Dev," said the old man.

Another boom from the Scrapyard's defences sounded awfully close.

"Winter Storm's here," said the Assessor, looking at his instruments. "It's time you were not."

THE WRECKING CREW

Mason gently nudged Aaron and gestured back the way the Collector had retreated.

"Let's go," he said quietly.

"What about this?" said Aaron, indicating to the X-ray tank, which another two guards were watching intently.

"We either stay here and hope we find what the Collector wants, or we destroy the bio-bot incubators. While they're still up and running, nobody stands a chance of getting in here to stop all of this."

They sidled away to the nearest shelving rack and quickly slipped out of view. Away from soldiers, they ran as fast as they could towards the other side of the Green Zone.

Aaron was already puffing for breath. "We can't just ... run and tell him to ... stop." He stopped and bent over with his hands on his knees as he caught his breath.

Mason stopped too and looked around the warehouse impatiently. Then something caught his eye.

"Aaron, I hate to agree with you ... but, yeah, we're not going to run in. We're going to enter in style."

The Collector stood before the incubator vats, which were already a quarter filled with writhing bio-bots suspended in a soup-like fluid. He was lost in thought as Eema rolled to his side.

"Winter Storm has located the target and is engaging in combat."

"Good. Capture Devon alive. See to it that the others are all destroyed."

"Yes, sir. The second Storm will be ready in twenty-three minutes."

"How are our prisoners?"

"Still in the medical bay," said Eema after a pause during which she accessed the security cameras.

"As soon as Winter Storm succeeds, get rid of them."
When no confirmation came, the Collector looked at
Eema. "Did you hear my command?"

"Something is coming. . ."

Sparks suddenly erupted across Eema's body. Her
voice became a series of electronic squeals, then faded to
silence. Her holographic head pixelated, then vanished.
Her spherical body rolled to the side as her stabilizers
powered down.

Before the Collector could say anything, the throaty
roar of a diesel engine echoed across the warehouse and,
with an enormous crash, Mason and Aaron's tank-like
vehicle smashed through the closest shelf, scattering
dozens of gadgets in every direction. It rolled on
caterpillar tracks, but it did not have a gun or artillery
barrel. The front was sleek and pointed like a stealth
fighter, with an enormous geodesic ball – like a golf
ball – attached to the back like a hunch. It was a rolling
electromagnetic pulse generator.

Mason was at the controls, yelling at the top of his
lungs as the tank smashed through the first vat – millions
of bio-bots surging to the floor, wriggling like maggots as
gallons of thick liquid poured out with them. The vat's
wafer-thin sides did nothing to slow the tank down.

The second vat was utterly destroyed in another torrent of bots and fluid as the tank punched through the base of the third, causing it to collapse with a tidal wave of gunk gushing across the floor in all directions.

The tank landed perfectly, bouncing twice before Mason was able to skid it in a U-turn and face the Collector. Aaron was sitting in the seat behind Mason, powering up another electromagnetic pulse strong enough to fry any electronics in the immediate area. Its range wasn't very broad, but was enough for the first pulse to disable the cameras and motion sensors within twenty metres so Eema hadn't detected them until it was too late. Now Eema and any electronic device the Collector had on him were disabled – as were the laser rifles of the four guards standing with him, as they found out, raising them to fire but just clicking the triggers uselessly.

Mason revved the engine, then drove across the piles of writhing, half-formed bio-bots – crushing them under the tracks with the satisfactory sound of millions of bubble-wrap bubbles popping. The tank slid as the bots were turned to mush. He brought the tank to a stop in an arc and popped the hatch open above the driver's seat. He stood up and looked at his handiwork with a smile.

"Looks like we crushed your plan!" Mason chuckled

at his own joke. The look of shock on the Collector's face made him laugh harder.

Finally, the Collector found his voice. "It looks as if I underestimated you, Mason."

"Most people do."

The Collector threw up his hands in surrender. He gave a nod to his guards, and they threw down their weapons and raised their hands too. Mason hoisted himself from the tank and Aaron passed him a ball of blue gel about the size of a tennis ball before following him out, carrying a similar gizmo.

Mason raised the ball threateningly. It was something he'd found on the shelf, another failed toy that had inadvertently become a dangerous weapon in a child's hand. The instructions read:

ICE-BLAST – SHAKE IT UP AND FREEZE YOUR FRIENDS!

"Care to tell us what you're looking for before we deep freeze you?"

"I was looking for Dev."

Mason tilted his head, confused. "You're looking in the wrong place. Dev isn't here."

"I assure you he is." The Collector lowered his arms. "I can show you."

Mason hesitated, but Aaron took a step forward. "No, you don't, pal. No mind games. Get those hands back up."

The Collector raised his hands again. "I'm only trying to help."

"No. You're trying to confuse." Aaron raised his Ice-Blast.

Then a voice from behind sent a shiver down both Mason and Aaron's spines. "No. He's trying to stall. Drop the gizmos *very* carefully."

The boys both crouched and carefully placed their Ice-Blasts on the floor before turning around and facing Onslow Winter.

"I have to say, I'm *very* disappointed with you," said Aaron, dropping his hands in defeat.

INTO THE
WILD BLACK
YONDER

"Launch in T-minus fifteen seconds," came the Assessor's voice over Dev's headset.

Dev checked his seat's harness was tight. He'd done so several times already, but it helped take his mind off what he had done to Lot and Riya. He wanted to press some button, just to *do* something, but the Assessor had warned him not to touch anything. The dials and buttons were all marked with Russian writing. The only one Dev needed to press was a switch that would lower the landing gear. As the writing under it had faded, Dev had marked the switch with a bright orange Post-it note. Just to do something, Dev pressed the note firmly, ensuring it was held in place.

The salvager robot team had carried the Buran shuttle into the Hyperloop tube, and carefully wrapped the long glider wings around the fuselage so it could fit into the tunnel. The Assessor had assured Dev they would unfold, like flower petals, once it had been fired out of the tube.

"Twelve seconds. . ."

The image of Lot crumpling to the floor with a confused and hurt expression on her face kept replaying in Dev's mind. . .

Then something occurred to him. He keyed his radio. "Doesn't the Hyperloop work in a vacuum?"

The Hyperloop was being hailed as mass transport that could get commuters to cities around the world, travelling in special trains at over seven hundred miles per hour. They had a similar transport system around the Inventory, although it hadn't been used for decades. Dev and his friends had once had an unfortunate incident in the vacuum tube.

"That's right," said the Assessor over the radio. "Electromagnetic suspension, essentially two pairs of super-magnets pushing away from one another – propel it forward in a vacuum. The lack of air resistance makes it go even faster."

The salvagers had created an electromagnetic sledge on which the Buran sat to serve the same purpose. Dev reacted when the Buran shuddered as the air was pumped out of the Hyperloop tunnel to create a vacuum.

"T-minus ten seconds..." said the Assessor.

Dev suddenly realized what was bothering him about the plan. He thumbed the radio. "If this tube is a vacuum, that means it's sealed both ends. I will be crashing through a solid wall on my way out."

"Don't worry about that," came the Assessor's distracted answer. Dev could hear shouting in the background, followed by several explosions.

"What's happening?"

"Winter Storm... Focus on your mission. Eight ... seven..."

"H-How's Lot?"

The Assessor's countdown paused. "She's still out cold."

Dev's throat felt dry. "Tell her..." He licked his dry lips. "Tell her I—"

"Launch."

There was no sound at all, but Dev was suddenly

thrust back in his chair as the shuttle accelerated atop the electromagnetic sledge. The view of the two-kilometre-long tunnel ahead didn't change at all. The end was depicted by a circular spot of black. The only sign he was moving was from the strip lighting rushing around the side of the tunnel.

The G-force crushed Dev against his seat, and it felt as if an elephant was sitting on his ribcage. He wasn't even able to raise his hand. If he angled his head slightly to look through the side windows, the G-force made his eyeballs go sideways. It was a horrible feeling. Using all his strength, he focused ahead.

And now he saw the dark circle at the end of the tunnel was racing towards him at an incredible speed. It was the enclosing wall.

As the very last second the wall blew apart from charges the salvagers had carefully planted. The Buran shot out of the inclined tunnel at seven hundred and fifty miles per hour, straight into the cyclone.

The immense winds rocked the shuttle, which creaked and groaned as the air pressure battered it. The glider wings unfurled and the ramjet engines activated immediately as air was sucked into them.

Dev felt another powerful kick as the shuttle was

lifted upwards with even more complaints from the aging fuselage. Dev tried to ignore the fact he had put his life in the hands of forty-year-old Russian engineering.

The flight details were programmed in the autopilot, so all Dev could do was hang on as the shuttle banked. Rain plastered the windscreen, so he could see very little ahead. Through the streams of water on the side window he caught a fleeting glimpse of the rolling scrapyard and flashes of explosions, before the storm clouds obscured everything.

Dev glanced at the altimeter and saw it was broken, the glass cracked. He could be certain of one thing though: he was going up.

The thud of rain suddenly turned to a ferocious clatter, like marbles dropping from the sky. The dark clouds outside were suddenly threaded with black, rope-like strands. Some shot past the shuttle; others hit the nose and stuck. Dev watched, mesmerized, as the strands started to crawl towards one another. They were bio-bots – and they were slowly forming Winter Storm.

Despite the storm winds, the speed of the shuttle and the powering rain, Dev watched as the figure of the blank-faced Winter Storm formed on the nose. Where its feet should be, strands of bio-bots snaked away like tree roots wrapping around the shuttle to anchor it in place.

"Dev to Scrap: Winter Storm is here!" Dev yelled into the radio mic strapped to his chin. "What do I do?"

The garbled reply came through, then ended with static. Dev cursed the antique radio equipment; there had been no time to update it, and the cyclone was causing interference. "Say again?" he shouted.

The Assessor's voice rose through the wash of static. "It's suddenly going. I think you're luring it away! Good job!"

Good job wasn't the response that Dev had hoped for. Strapped to his seat, there was very little he could do except watch.

The tendrils holding the figure in place grew thicker as more bio-bots flew to join it. Winter Storm slid its feet along the Buran's nose so it could draw closer to the cockpit window. It pulled back a fist and froze in place. For a second, Dev thought the bio-machine had short-circuited . . . but that was wishful thinking. Its fist was becoming larger, ballooning as more bio-bots were ushered towards it, until it was the size of Dev's head.

Then Winter Storm punched the glass.

The thud was so jarring that it echoed around the shuttle. Dev realized he had closed his eyes – and when he didn't feel the blast of wind on his face, he dared to open them...

Amazingly, the old triple-glazed windscreen had held, although he saw a tiny crack in the corner of the outer pane. Winter Storm drew his fist back again and power-drove it with another mighty thump. This time the outer pane shattered.

Dev's heart skipped a beat as Winter Storm readied for another blow. With only two panes of glass between him and certain death, he had to do something...

Then they were suddenly out of the storm and rising faster than a bullet. Ahead the sky was a dark blue as they approached the edge of space. Winter Storm had been bracing itself against the ferocious cyclone winds and now, without them, it overcompensated and staggered sideways.

Dev hoped it would slip off the edge of the craft, but instead Winter Storm revolved around the nose cone, like a ring twisting around a finger – held on by the tendrils from its feet that now encircled the shuttle.

The Buran shimmied as tiny thrusters around the nose kicked into action to flip it over before it broke through the atmosphere. The roll was a standard manoeuvre, and it gave Dev two benefits.

The first was the view of the Earth below and behind him, but as he inverted he could see it fill the top of the cockpit window. He wondered if he was the only teenager to not be bothered seeing the planet from orbit for the second time in as many weeks. However, the circular dirty-grey swirl of clouds that formed the cyclone looked almost beautiful, with the eye of the storm clearly visible.

The second benefit came as Winter Storm crawled back around the nose cone to reach the windscreen just as another pair of thrusters fired to stop the roll — one of which was placed under the stream of bio-bots anchoring Winter Storm in place.

While the tiny bio bots seemed able to survive the cold of space, those placed directly over the thruster were incinerated by the heat, and those immediately around it melted. No longer safely held in place, Winter Storm dropped to its knees and dug its fingers into the fuselage, ripping metal.

But it wasn't quick enough.

Nagging at the back of Dev's mind had been the fact that the ramjets required air to function, and this high up, the rarefied atmosphere meant there was almost nothing to power them. He recalled the Assessor mumbling something about modified boosters, but had been distracted by telling Fabian his plan to subdue Lot and Riya, so he hadn't really listened.

A tremendous boom rattled the Buran, and Dev's bones. Then the shuttle shot forward as the rear boosters ignited for the final thrust into space.

Dev had watched the salvagers fill the shuttle's cargo hold with a large liquid fuel tank and now understood that it was providing the final kick. He tried to raise his hands so he could use his synaesthesia to communicate with the ship, but the G-forces once again held him back, his palms pinned against his legs.

Outside, Winter Storm was thrust against the glass – some bio-bots splattering like bugs on the windscreen – and then it was gone as the bio-bot was torn from the shuttle and sent spiralling back down into the storm below.

The shuttle shook so hard that parts of the aging trim inside began to fall off. Then, just as suddenly as it had begun, the boosters stopped. Dev felt a wave of panic – had they broken? Run out of fuel? Without them he would plummet straight back to Earth and there would be nothing to catch him. Outside the windscreen he could see nothing but darkness. . .

Then small items of trim floated past him, caught in microgravity. He was in orbit! Dev sighed deeply and unclipped his seat belt. He floated up from his seat. Once again, the novelty of being weightless was lost on him. He was still having nightmares of fighting Lee in zero gravity just weeks ago.

The thrusters kicked in to correct the Buran's course. With the Earth behind him and only darkness ahead, Dev crossed his fingers that he had enough oxygen to reach his destination. Despite his own impending doom, his thoughts drifted back to Lot and that stolen kiss.

He dreaded what she would think about it when she woke up.

ONE-WAY TICKET

Lot woke to find she was lying next to Riya in a room that was shaking from the hurricane. It had once been part of a Winnebago motorhome and the Assessor had cut it up to use as a wing of his home, so it was hardly the strongest of buildings.

She hurried to the window in time to witness the end of the battle, as the raging winds were preventing Winter Storm from forming as an effective weapon. Through the driving rain and banshee winds she watched as the swarm of bio-bots took to the air to pursue Dev's shuttle.

Riya woke moments later, just as Fabian and the Assessor hurried inside.

"And how are you, ladies?" Fabian asked sheepishly.

He was answered with a punch as Riya sat up. "Do that to either of us again and you'll be more than sorry!" She would have gone for the Assessor too if he had been within reach.

Fabian quickly retreated, rubbing his jaw with one hand and holding the other up to stop any further assault.

"I'm sorry! But it had to be done or you would have interfered with Dev's voyage."

"I hate him!" snarled Lot, kicking a small bedside table. "I struggled to trust you before, but from now on, consider yourself a permanent enemy."

Fabian opened his mouth to answer but stopped when he saw the Assessor quickly shake his head, warning him not to argue back.

Lot gazed out of the window, watching the patterns made by the rain. "Whose idea was it?"

The Assessor blew out a long breath before answering. "It was Dev's." Lot looked at him, weighing up whether or not to believe him. "Based on sound data. There isn't enough oxygen on-board the Buran for all three of you. And once you are up there, you would be unable to get back down."

"What's that supposed to mean?"

An uneasy silence descended, broken only by the wind and rain. Finally, Fabian sighed and spoke up.

"It means that —" he pointed up "— the shuttle only had a one-way ticket."

Lot gave a sharp intake of breath, but squeezed her fists tightly to stop any unwelcome tears. She stared at Fabian, her jaw muscles almost cramping with tension as she allowed Fabian to continue.

"The point of the Inventory's backup was as a remote storage facility. I'm sure there are plenty of vehicles up there that he can use to get home."

"And he can get some oxygen there and use the shuttle to return," Riya pointed out as she rubbed her sore knuckles.

The Assessor waved his hand dismissively. "A piece of junk that barely made orbit. So many heat-shield tiles fell off, it would burn up on re-entry."

Fabian chipped in before the girls could speak: "And he only went up for a specific reason — to infiltrate the Inventory. To get in there, stop the Collector and hopefully save Mason and Aaron."

Riya snorted. "How can he do that from up there?"

"I imagine he's thinking of employing the Eternal Machine," said Fabian. "Uploading himself into a body back at the original Inventory. It's the perfect way to sneak inside."

Lot scowled. "So to do that, will he . . . die in space? I can't. . ." She closed her eyes and shook her head. "And what part do Riya and I play in this rescue plan?"

The Assessor broke into a broad smile. "Ah! I have some good news for you about that. Your parts have been played. You both get to stay here and be safe. We can't afford to lose any more members of the team."

"That's good to know," said Lot with a sigh of relief. She managed a smile . . . then swapped a look with Riya. A look they both understood: *no chance.*

"You know, throughout your whole confession, I had secretly hoped you were just being remotely controlled," said Aaron, unable to hide the disappointment in his voice. "But now I think Mase was right. You really are just one of the bad guys."

Onslow Winter stepped closer, the small device in his hand kept squarely pointed at both boys. Mason recognized it as a dimensionalizer, the Collector's weapon of choice before the World Consortium arrested him. One false move and he and Aaron would be smothered in nanoparticles and flattened into two dimensions.

"I told you I should have died a long time ago from a crippling disease that was eating me from the inside," Winter said with a shrug. He held up his hand so they could see the bio-bots wriggle under his skin. "They replaced the bits of me that were dying."

Aaron frowned. "So, if those things are keeping you alive, then that makes you a cyborg. Half human, half machine."

Winter grinned. "I'm so much more than a cyborg. My bio-bots are a living machine."

"A bio-borg," said Mason sarcastically.

Winter nodded. "Exactly. You see, all those other bio-bots —" he indicated to the crushed mess on the floor "— and the ones currently killing all your friends . . ." He paused just long enough to savour the upset looks on their faces. ". . . are being controlled. And who controls remote-controlled people? Haven't you wondered who was pulling all the strings?" He jiggled his arms up and down like a marionette puppet.

"You're controlling Winter Storm?" said Aaron slowly.

Winter rolled his eyes. "Man! I *am* Winter Storm." He tapped his head. "With a superior bio-processor. Tech still ain't beaten the old human noggin." He looked over their shoulders to the Collector, who had one hand pressed against his earpiece. "So, what do you want me to do with these leftovers?"

The Collector removed his hand from his ear. Mason swore he saw uncertainty flicker across his face, but then the villain gave a thin smile. "I was going to dispose of them, but now I think they deserve to be let in on a little secret."

"What's that, then? That you suffer very bad BO?" said Mason, wafting a hand in front of his nose. "I have to tell you, that's no secret." The Collector's brief look of doubt was enough to reassure him that his friends were not only alive and well, but something hadn't gone according to plan.

"We have located the Black Zone," the Collector said simply. "Now you are going to see what your so-called friends have been keeping from you."

He turned on his heel and marched away with his guard flanking him. Mason felt Winter push him in the small of the back to force him to follow.

"Move it, and don't try anything. I'm not quite as merciful as he is."

Mason and Aaron followed, and they were both thinking the same thing: When was help finally going to come?

LILITH

An old grey cathode-ray monitor with its curved grey screen blinked to life with a vector line animation depicting what Dev could only assume was his destination. Russian Cyrillic text appeared on another screen with two words flashing urgently, complete with a rasping alarm. He had no idea what they meant.

He lightly tapped into the Buran's computers using his synaesthesia, to see if he could convince the system to display in English. Unfortunately, there was no such option, and he could only override it. At least he managed to silence the alarm.

"Dev to Scrap: I'm coming up on Lilith now, I

think," he said through the radio. He still hadn't heard back from the scrapyard and hoped the storm was still scrambling the radio. Any other explanation was too dire to think about.

He wasn't sure how long he had been travelling. There was no clock, and the position of Lilith meant that it orbited in perpetual daylight, so there was little sense of passing time from the Earth below. The air was beginning to taste sour, which was a sign the Assessor had warned him would mean he was running out of breathable air and the cabin was slowly filling with poisonous carbon dioxide. Each of his breaths expelled more deadly gas, and the build-up was already beginning to fog his senses. Only the small cockpit was pressurized, not the rest of the Buran, and Fabian had calculated it would have *just* enough air for the mission.

Provided nothing went wrong. Dev's eyes darted to the broken windscreen. So far, the remaining two panes were holding.

Providing Fabian's calculations were correct.

There was a black spot ahead. Dev's first instinct was to wipe the glass, but no, it was Lilith, precisely where the archaic Russian computer had predicted. With the sunlight behind it, it was never visible from the Earth, but up here Dev could see the small, irregularly shaped moon.

The Buran's autopilot fired the thrusters, repositioning the spacecraft for its final approach. The Assessor had told him there was nothing for him to do but sit tight. Within moments Lilith filled the cockpit window. Although it looked massive, Dev had to remind himself it was only the size of Great Britain, which was minuscule on a planetary scale.

There was a gentle shudder as Lilith's weak gravity took hold and Dev gently descended to the floor. He scrambled into the pilot's seat, strapped himself in, and his hands hovered uselessly over the control stick.

As the shuttle fell into orbit over the moon's permanently lit side, Dev could now see a huge dome just like the one from his uncle's dream. A few gasps from the navigational thrusters lined the Buran up with a runway that ended in a hangar door that automatically rumbled open as Dev approached.

So far, so good. Dev reached out for the landing gear switch that he had marked with the orange Post-it note.

The note wasn't there!

A flash of orange to the side caught his attention.

The note was now stuck to the ceiling. It must have jarred loose during the launch and he hadn't noticed. Now he was faced with a panel of toggle switches – and the Cyrillic writing had rubbed off most of them. He hovered his hand over the switch he thought it was, but hesitated. Pressing the wrong thing at this stage could be fatal, and the built-up carbon dioxide was making him feel sleepy. If he succumbed to sleep, he would never wake up again.

Instead he gently rested his hand on a switch and used his gift to feel his way through to the landing gear system and instructed it to lower itself. He felt the wash of electronics that assured him the task had been complete, but the ship was worryingly quiet. The landing gear was a series of heavy-duty hydraulic pistons, so they should be making a racket as they lowered ... which meant they were not working, despite what the electronics were telling Dev.

"Ah, Scrap, we have a problem," he said into the radio. He briefly paused, hoping for a response. A final hiss from the thrusters nudged the shuttle for the perfect approach. "Scrap, if you can hear me, I'm crash-landing – and not by choice!"

He gripped the control stick with white knuckles.

With the autopilot on there was no way he could steer the shuttle, but it gave him a sense of security. The shuttle's belly scraped against the runway with a sound that made Dev's teeth jangle. More trim, bolts and panels fell from the roof and walls and floated down with the urgency of a snowflake.

Thanks to the lack of air, there were no sparks; otherwise the entire shuttle may have gone up in flames. The hangar door was still slowly opening as the Buran approached. Special forward-facing thrusters in the nose automatically fired to slow the shuttle's approach. To his horror, Dev saw only the thrusters on the starboard side fired; the opposite pair must have been damaged by Winter Storm.

The shuttle began to slew sideways and showed no signs of slowing. Dev slapped his hands against the computer screen, forcing his synaesthesia to trick the port-side thruster into firing. They refused to respond. Dev weighed up his options. . .

He had none.

He looked up in time to see the Buran had turned a full forty-five degrees while continuing to slide forward as the hangar door opened *just enough* for the shuttle to slide under. The cockpit was the first to enter an empty airlock the size of a football pitch – but the body had twisted too far and slammed into the side of the hangar door at speed.

The Buran was decapitated. The side of the hangar severed the cockpit from the fuselage just a metre behind the airlock that was protecting Dev from the rest of the shuttle. Flying debris filled the low-gravity atmosphere like a dense swarm of flies.

The cockpit rapidly spun into the hangar before toppling over and slowly rolling a dozen times towards the far wall. Inside, the first impact was so severe it jolted every bone in Dev's body. He unlocked his seat belt and pushed himself free as the cockpit began to roll. Suspended in the microgravity, the cabin rolled around him like a washing machine – but Dev remained unaffected.

The hangar sensors detected an emergency and the doors slammed down, shredding the rest of the Buran's fuselage just as the cockpit crashed into the wall.

Dev was saved by a second as the hangar was flooded with oxygen almost instantly. The cockpit cracked open around Dev like an egg, the windscreen shattering. Dev tasted the clear air that revived his foggy senses, enough for him to be able to crawl from the wreckage.

However, now filled with oxygen, the sparking cockpit and fuselage suddenly caught fire. In the blink of an eye, a curtain of orange flames consumed both the cockpit and the wreckage strewn across the room.

"That was close," Dev muttered to himself. He gulped in the hangar's icy cold pure air and watched as thick black smoke pooled above him. He didn't think it was a good idea to wait around much longer. He clambered to his feet and tried to walk to the door, which was difficult in the low gravity. Remembering his time on-board Black Knight, he stopped trying to walk normally and instead bounded in a series of kangaroo leaps to the only other exit.

He was halfway across when he suddenly became aware of a rising whistle. His head snapped around to the source – it was coming from the main hangar door. The air was leaking out. Even at a distance, he could see the burning wreckage pinned under the door was warping the airtight seal. As he watched, the clouds of black smoke suddenly funnelled from the roof towards the leak in a long, thin tornado.

"Oh, rats..." he said under his breath as he instinctively tried to run. Once again, the low gravity made him stumble, losing him precious seconds. He fell forward in slow motion, his arms flailing, and it felt as if he would never catch his balance *or* hit the floor.

Then there was a loud crack from the hangar door and Dev was suddenly yanked sideways as the air was sucked at hurricane speeds through a broken seal no larger than a marble. The burning shuttle debris shot across the room and smashed against the door. Dev's fingers scraped along the floor as he was pulled feet first towards the breach. . .

Then, just as suddenly as it began, the tempest stopped as the debris sealed the hole. But the wind had fuelled the flames and now, bunched together, they burned with an inferno-like rage.

Dev knew it was only a matter of seconds, not minutes, before the blaze melted a hole through the door. On all fours, he loped towards the exit. Faced with a palm scanner to unlock it, he used his gift to bypass the security. The door slid open and Dev slowly fell into the corridor beyond. The door snapped back in place just as the weakened outer hangar door finally failed.

Through the small portal in the door, Dev saw the remains of the Buran and every item within the hangar get sucked out into the vacuum of Lilith's hostile landscape.

There was no time to congratulate himself for a lucky escape: he had wasted enough time already. With another deep breath to clear his mind, he took in his new environment.

The immaculate pure white corridor curved away to the left and right, and he supposed that it followed the perimeter of the dome he had seen from outside. The junction ahead sloped upwards to what he hoped was the control centre.

NO ONE LEFT BEHIND

The Assessor peered through the window, then consulted a screen on his chair. "That's the worst of it over."

The wind had died down to something more manageable after the cyclone passed, and the rain no longer fell horizontally. Lot and Riya were sitting at a table nursing warm drinks, impatiently watching a display screen that seemed to have come from the 1970s for any signal from the Buran. Riya slapped the side of the monitor just in case it improved reception.

"I can't believe with all this technology around us we still can't get a decent signal in a storm!"

Fabian had been holding his mobile phone aloft, trying to get connected. He nodded in agreement. "Mother Nature is still a force to be respected. . ."

A beep from the Assessor's computer made them all look up like meerkats.

"Ah, that's the defence network. No sign of Winter Storm. I think the cyclone must have disposed of it."

"Or the bio-bots found Dev. . ." Lot said morosely.

The Assessor tried his most placating tone; he was not used to talking to people so young. "The backup site has no direct channels of communication. Unless Dev chooses to move one of the dishes up there to focus on us, we're out of contact. That was the whole point in making it secret and isolated. You can't see it, there are no signals . . . and only a handful of people know about it. We can only hope he's not dead. We don't know enough about the Eternal Machine to know whether he – or some version of him – could be brought back."

That possibility did little to cheer up Lot. The Assessor cleared his throat and laid a hand on her shoulder.

"What he's trying to say is it is very likely Dev is there already. The autopilot would have taken care of everything. All he had to do was sit back and enjoy the ride."

Lot shucked off his hand. "So we just sit here and do nothing?"

The Assessor flinched as a sudden gust of wind buckled the metal wall of what had once been a Portakabin. He quickly composed himself. "The Collector knows of this place, so there is no telling when he will strike again. You two need to go somewhere safe."

"Where?"

Fabian beamed. "You are to come back to Company House with me."

Lot slowly stood up. "Like prisoners?"

The aghast look on the old man's face almost made her laugh. "Nothing of the sort! Like the guests you are." He indicated to the Assessor. "If anything, as a man from the Company, I am the prisoner."

The Assessor nodded to the girls. "I assure you, once we get the Inventory back, you'll be free to go." He glanced at Fabian. "You too."

Lot didn't like the sound of "free to go", but said nothing. It was Riya who spoke up.

"And if we don't get it back?"

The Assessor and Fabian exchanged glances. "Then you may well be in the only safe place left in this world."

*

Still caught in the tail of the storm, Fabian was hesitant about using the Company's teleport system, which required clear skies. Lot and Riya had weighed in, saying they didn't want to chance losing parts of their anatomy, although the real reason was that they were in no hurry to become Fabian's prisoners.

Fabian settled on using a dart-shaped aircraft the Assessor had stored in a remote area of the scrapyard. It was another relic from the Russian's Cold War armoury, a modified Tupolev TU-144. It was a supersonic aircraft – so, not as fast as Lot was used to with the Avro – which had been made as a rival to the West's now-scrapped Concorde. It looked almost the same except that the military had inserted a cargo ramp at the back of the plane. The comfortable passenger seats had been removed and replaced with jump seats bolted to the inside of the hull to face one another and offer more cargo space.

Lot and Riya hugged the Assessor goodbye, then pushed aside various items of junk. None of it would have come with the original aircraft; instead the fuselage had obviously been used as a storage dump. There was a rusting snowmobile chained to the floor, a couple of triangular surfboards fastened to cargo webbing on the wall and a crate of what looked like party horns which they couldn't fathom how they got on-board an aging Russian jet in a top-secret scrapyard in Bangladesh.

As they took their seats it turned out that, in his youth, Fabian had been a test pilot and was more than adept at flying the Tupolev. The sleek shape of the aircraft was perfect for slicing effortlessly through the clouds, and they were soon at cruising speed. Riya closed her eyes to sleep while Lot unclipped her seat belt and dug around the junk in the back.

After a couple of hours or so, she visited Fabian on the flight deck. He looked out of place, dressed smartly in tweed, and sat behind chunky military hardware from the 1970s. She noted they were travelling just under Mach 2, and the altimeter read eighty thousand feet, almost three times higher than an average passenger jet.

"How's it going?"

Fabian stifled a yawn and nodded to a paper map folded on the seat next to him. The Tupolev was too old to have a GPS system.

"We're on course. About here." He tapped the map. "Still a couple of hours to go, but we are at the top of our climb."

Lot yawned. "OK. We're going to try and sleep."

"Lucky you." Fabian was distracted as he checked the flight instruments.

Lot gently closed the cockpit door. Then she looped a rubber hose that had been lying around, wrapping it around the slide lever that locked the door. She knotted the other end of the tube to a hanging strap that the crew could hold during turbulence. She knew the tube would stretch, but not by enough to let Fabian exit the cockpit.

She hurried across to Riya and shook her awake. Riya looked around with a start, expecting trouble.

"What's going on?"

"We're leaving."

Riya rubbed her eyes and stretched. "Are we there already?"

"No. We're eight thousand angels above the ground —" she automatically adopted the pilot's slang her father used "— and this is our stop." She threw an olive-green jumpsuit at Riya.

Riya looked uncomprehendingly at the suit, then at Lot. "Wait a second, I must have missed a step here. This isn't a bus where you ring a bell and jump off."

"It's kind of the same," said Lot. "But without the bell."

Riya examined the jumpsuit. "This is a pressurized suit."

"Yup." Lot had already stepped into the feet of her suit and was pulling it over her own clothes. Designed to fit an adult, her extra clothing now meant it fitted snugly and would provide an extra layer of warmth. Riya unbuckled her seat belt and started to put her suit on.

"You have a plan, right?"

"Sort of," said Lot as she zipped the suit up. She tossed a helmet to Riya, an old fighter pilot's with an enclosed faceplate and a small oxygen bottle hanging from the end of a hose. "There should be enough air in that to last twelve minutes."

Riya traced her finger over the scuffed and faded hammer-and-sickle logo on the side of the helmet.

"I dread to ask, but what will we be doing for twelve minutes?"

"Surfing!"

Lot picked up one of the delta-shaped boards she had seen on the way in. She had immediately recognized them as a variant sky-board, a gadget she had once pleaded with Charles Parker to let them try. He had absolutely refused, stating they were too dangerous ... which was ironic, considering the rest of the tech inside the Inventory.

Riya zipped up her suit and carefully rotated the

board. It was similar to a snowboard, but the end fanned out, forming tiny wings. A pair of foot clamps were bolted on the upper side to hold the rider in place.

"So we . . . jump out and surf clouds?"

Lot helped Riya strap a parachute to her back. "For a bit, yeah, then pull the cord and float down the rest of the way on this." Lot placed her foot on Riya's so she could yank the parachute's strap tight. Even a few millimetres' wriggle room from a loose strap could cause an injury.

"I've never parachuted before," said Riya with a tremor of fright she had been trying so hard to conceal. She was in awe of Lot's confidence, and knew she had been parachuting many times with her parents.

"Nothing to it. Watch me. At three thousand feet —" Lot indicated to an altimeter built into the wrist of Riya's jumpsuit arm "— you pull this." She tapped a tarnished silver ring on the front of the parachute harness. "And this opens." She patted the parachute. Riya wasn't reassured when a cloud of dust rose from the chute.

Lot put on her own chute and carried the air-board to the end of the cargo ramp. She helped Riya secure her feet in the clamps.

"It's just like surfing," Lot assured her.

"I've never surfed before either!"

"Skateboarding?" Riya nodded. "Same difference, except it will hurt a whole lot more if you fall off." Lot's laugh was far from reassuring.

"Where are we going?"

Lot glanced at her watch. "We're not far from the Inventory. The speed and height we're going, we can get pretty close. Just follow my lead." She secured Riya's face mask before she could ask another question, and put her hand on the button to open the ramp. "We're moving at supersonic speeds — faster than sound. I don't know if anybody has ever done a jump like this before."

She saw Riya's eyes widen behind her visor, and a muffled chorus of swearing. Lot smiled as she heaved away the metal bolt across the door and hit the button. A red light flashed and a warning klaxon echoed through the cargo hold. She silently thanked the lack of safety features aboard the Soviet jet.

"It should be fun!" She secured her own mask.

With a heavy clunk, the ramp suddenly descended, and before they had time to do anything, they were sucked out of the plane and into the supersonic wake of the aircraft.

THE BACKUP

As he made his way along the corridor, Dev marvelled that everything looked so clean and new, as if it had only just been built. He imagined the Inventory, the original, must have once looked similar. The door ahead spiralled open and Dev bounced into a circular control room that was identical to the one he had stood in during his uncle's dream. The view through the panoramic windows was the same barren grey landscape with a star-peppered sky from horizon to horizon.

But he wasn't here to admire the view. He moved to the nearest computer terminal and accessed it through his fingertips. He didn't need to look at the screen to see a map of this new Inventory site; it appeared in his mind's eye and was almost a mirror image of the one far below on Earth.

Within seconds he had located the device he was looking for: the TelePath Inductor. It was the machine that sucked memories from people and allowed them to be stored and experienced in the TelePath.

The Assessor had given him clear instructions; it was the backup of the device that Charles Parker was using in the Inventory to put Dev's memories, his entire personality, into a new cloned body. And that's exactly what Dev planned to use it for.

He memorized the location and hurried to the elevator.

Dev had to pinch himself to check he still wasn't inside Charles Parker's dream. The Green Zone looked almost identical to the one he knew, except it was brand new. The shelves were packed with thousands of gadgets, stretching into the distance. It was as he remembered the Inventory before the Collector had originally broken in.

Painfully aware that time was against him and that his friends' lives were on the line, Dev didn't linger. But he had to take care walking in the low gravity; if he moved too quickly he would catapult himself into a solid wall at speed. Then a thought struck him: if this was a mirror image of the old Inventory. . .

He hopped to a nearby shelf and ran his hand over the items stored on their own personalized plinths. He couldn't help but repress a smile as he found what he was looking for.

"Hello, you beauties. . ."

In less than thirty seconds, Dev was quickly flying through the long aisles using the bulky HoverBoots strapped to his feet. He covered the distance across the Green Zone without incident and found the TelePath Inductor.

It was much bigger than he had expected. Telepaths implanted thoughts and memories, and they were small earpieces; instead, the machine before him was about the size of a house. Huge, imposing metal coils were arranged in a fan, all pointing towards a single chair in the centre of the machine. Based on what he knew from the Inventory equipment, it would probably need several technicians to operate it, but in the staff-less backup site, Dev would have to rely on his synaesthesia.

Powering up the machine and connecting it to Lilith's communications satellite dish took almost thirty minutes as he followed a precise set of instructions from a digital manual stored within the machine. He locked on to a secure signal that beamed directly to the inventory. Then he sat in the chair and used his power to initiate the Inductor.

He closed his eyes. The image of Lot's smile appeared, and he regretted never saying goodbye. He wondered what she was doing right now... He forced his mind clear. He was sure, whatever she was doing, that she was safe.

He took a deep breath.

It would be his very last.

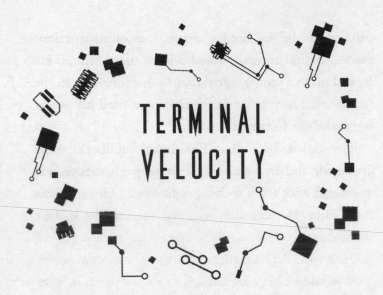

TERMINAL VELOCITY

Brains have the most wonderful techniques for dealing with extreme circumstances by blotting out the danger and focusing on the unusual.

As Lot tumbled from an aircraft travelling at almost twice the speed of sound, she marvelled that she could still hear her own screams at eighty thousand feet above the ground.

Riya tumbled below her, rolling head over heels out of control as they fell from the supersonic aircraft. This high up, there was almost no air, so there was little resistance to slow Lot, but she still needed more speed. Straining every muscle, she pulled herself flat against the board, making herself as flat as possible to allow her to scythe through the air. She angled the board downwards, gaining on Riya.

Lot drew alongside her friend, now both falling at the same speed. She grabbed hold of Riya to stop her turning – but instead was yanked forward, rolling through the air herself. This simple act – combined with the air thickening with every metre they dropped – slowed them down to mere terminal velocity.

With some effort, she held on to Riya with one hand and steadied them both by extending the other to catch their balance. She peered at Riya and saw her eyes were wide with fear. Lot gave her the "OK" gesture ... then noticed Riya had been sick in her own helmet.

She looked away. They were so high the curvature of the planet was obvious. The Tupolev had been moving so quickly that it was already out of sight as they fell. The sky above was inky black, and Lot pondered what Dev was doing right now...

No. She had to concentrate on the task at hand. Below them the continent spread out, and Lot was thankful she had always been interested in geography. You never knew when it would come in handy to find your way home. Especially when free-falling at one hundred and fifty miles per hour. Still holding on to Riya with one hand, she pointed in the direction they needed to travel, and soared them gracefully through the air.

It was a whole five minutes of falling, constantly slowed by their air-boards and air resistance as the atmosphere became thicker. A quick look at her altimeter showed they had fallen thirty thousand feet.

Several more minutes ticked past, and Lot was enjoying every moment. As the air resistance increased, she moved away from Riya so she could get used to solo-surfing. At first Riya's arms windmilled around to catch her balance, but she quickly got the hang of it. Lot was impressed; it was amazing what motivation a face full of vomit gave people.

Another few minutes ticked past, and now there was so much wind resistance on the board that they were both being forced into a crouch position like traditional surfers. Lot had snowboarded many times, so couldn't resist pulling a few rolls and loops, giggling with delight each time. She was so distracted that she didn't see Riya was frantically waving her arms and pointing to her mask.

Lot's instincts drew her attention to her own oxygen level on the canister. It was almost empty! She had probably used too much air by cheering and yelping as she performed her stunts – Riya had probably been screaming most of the way down so had exhausted hers too. She checked her altitude – thirty thousand feet. The height of Mount Everest, and the air was still too thin to breathe. If they didn't hurry, they would both suffocate before they landed.

Lot swooped into Riya's side again and grabbed her tightly. She slid the tip of her air-board over Riya's and wagged a forefinger, hoping her friend would interpret that as *get ready*. With no further warning, Lot leaned forward, pitching all her weight on the end of the boards so they pointed almost vertically down.

Without the wind resistance, they instantly plummeted earthward, rapidly gaining speed to two hundred miles per hour. Lot glanced at her altimeter as it whizzed down past twenty-five thousand feet. They were out of the notorious *death zone* where the air was too thin to breathe.

She looked back up in time to see a flash of silver in their path – and to her horror realized it was a passenger jet!

Renewing her grip on Riya, she barrel-rolled them to the side – just in time. They passed within metres of the aircraft, which roared past, leaving a wake of severe turbulence that sent them spinning again. But the plane was gone in an instant.

Lot slackened her face mask just enough to admit a blast of fresh, icy air in, but not wide enough that she'd be choked by the wind. She did the same for Riya, and tried to ignore the gloop that poured out.

The clouds beneath them were obscuring their target area, so Lot had no choice but to guess. At this height, they could still easily overshoot the Inventory by fifty miles.

As they plummeted through soft grey clouds, moisture instantly covered their jumpsuits and visors. Lot's gloves became so slick she lost grip with Riya – who tumbled into the murk.

Lot angled her air-board to slow her descent – it was like applying a brake. She slowed so quickly she was pushed to her knees, and forced to hold on to the front of the board with both hands.

Then she was out of the clouds and the ground filled her vision. She was relieved to see she was on target. The town where she lived lay to one side, then the rolling fields and farmland could be seen stretching into the distance and hiding the secretive Inventory beneath.

Riya was a mile away, no more than a tiny figure, but it appeared as if she had finally gained control of the board. She steadily curved towards Lot and, when she was close enough, gave her a double thumbs up. She was finally getting the hang of it.

After another minute Lot signalled to Riya that they should pull their chutes. Riya did so first, the oblong parachute springing from her pack and unfolding without a hitch. Lot blew out a sigh of relief and pulled her own ripcord.

Nothing happened.

She yanked it again and the frayed cord snapped. Her hand automatically went to her belly, where the emergency chute would normally be.

Normally.

She didn't have one. This wasn't a safely arranged jump that her father was leading; it had been an improvised affair with no thought of safety. And now she was about to pay the ultimate price.

Riya could only watch helplessly as Lot plummeted towards the Earth...

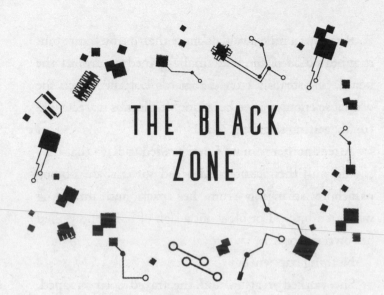

THE BLACK
ZONE

"Turncoat?" Aaron suggested as he was shoved in the small of his back by an irritated guard who, like the others, had retrieved new working weapons from the Inventory's cache.

Mason nodded. "Not bad. How about back-stabber?"

They had been coming up with synonyms for *traitor* as they followed the Collector and Onslow Winter to the other end of the Green Zone. Each suggestion had further agitated the tech entrepreneur.

"Will you both shut up?"

"Ooh! Ooh! Collaborator!" said Aaron gleefully.

Winter whirled around, raising his hand threateningly.

Bio-bots surged out of his skin and formed a long spike that wavered between Aaron's eyes. "One more word and it will be your last. You call me a *traitor*, while you are down here surrounded by all this technology. Tech that could be used to make people's lives better. How does that make you the good guys?"

"This stuff is dangerous," Mason pointed out – then sucked in his breath as the spike whipped in front of him.

"Everything can be dangerous in the wrong hands," Winter growled. "What this planet needs is a new world order, a fresh way of doing things. Shadow Helix failed, the Company failed and the World Consortium failed. We can make a difference."

"By taking everything over?"

"Think about it. No countries, no feuds, no wars. Why can't you see that's a much better place to live?"

Mason could see that Onslow Winter meant every word. He glanced at the Collector, who hadn't said a word. He couldn't bring himself to believe the Collector was doing all this in order to make the world a better place.

Ahead, the X-ray tank had stopped next to a section of wall that looked no different from any other. Norman the technician waited nervously, under the watchful eye of his two guards.

"Where is it?" the Collector demanded without breaking his stride.

Norman pointed to a chalk line he had made on the wall. The Collector stopped a few feet from the wall and squinted. After a moment he broke into a smile.

"Ah, I see it now. Charles Parker carefully shielded this from me." He clicked his fingers and indicated to the wall. "Open it up!"

All four guards put down their weapons and picked up heavy pneumatic drills, the sort used on road repairs. They made short work of the concrete wall, revealing a door beneath which they smashed through, exposing a corridor beyond. A waft of cool air blew over them.

"The Black Zone..." whispered the Collector in awe. He turned to Mason and Aaron. "Now you will see. Come."

They stepped into a hexagonal corridor that sloped sharply down. Motion-activated lights illuminated as their footsteps echoed on the metal floor. It was much more basic than the rest of the Inventory and had obviously been added later.

"What's down here?" asked Mason, walking alongside

the Collector. Aaron kept behind with Norman while the guards and Winter brought up the rear.

"A secret Charles Parker didn't want you to know about."

It felt as if they had descended several levels before they reached a junction. The Collector didn't pause as he turned left. After a few metres the junction ended at a door that had been left partially open.

Beyond was a large room with pipes and cables snaking across the floor and ceiling, all leading to three cryogenic pods suspended from the ceiling. One was open and empty, but Mason could see shadowy figures in the other two. From the lights on the controls, Mason guessed the occupants were still alive, but the Collector had no interest in them and continued on.

"Why are there frozen people down here?" whispered Aaron.

Mason shook his head, but gasped when he caught the name written on an empty pod: Stephan Ebert. "That was Tyker's original name!"

The Collector headed straight for a door on the left-hand side of the room. This too had been left ajar. The fiend couldn't stifle his excitement as they passed into a larger room.

"Behold, the Eternal Machine."

Whatever Mason had expected to find, it wasn't an aisle of glass tanks, each with a familiar figure suspended in the cryogenic fluid. He leaned close to Aaron.

"This has just taken a serious turn for the weird."

The Collector gestured like a showman. "You see, Dev *is* Iron Fist. He is the security lock, which means I can't get a single item out of the Inventory without him — well, not one that works, anyway. The items would self-destruct on the way out. But I don't need *your* Dev. Just *a* Dev. Ah, good old father. He always kept a spare key under the doormat . . . so to speak."

Mason still couldn't take his eyes from the Dev clones suspended in the containers. "All of this, just so you can use a clone to get everything out?"

"There is no need to empty the house now I have the keys. The Inventory and everything in it is wholly mine. Including its most precious treasure."

Aaron frowned, trying to play catch-up. As a new recruit, he hadn't been told about Dev being a clone, yet the evidence was right in front of him. "You mean Dev?"

The Collector laughed. "No. Not Dev. This." He gestured around the room. "The Eternal Machine. Pulling the mind from the body." He tapped his head.

"Then downloading it into a new and improved one."
He gestured to the clones. "Immortality. One could live
for ever without fear of death. Without aging. What is
the point in ruling the world if you are merely mortal?"

The horrific realization of the Collector's plan settled
on Mason's shoulders.

"You don't just want to control the planet. You want
to do it *for ever*."

The Collector raised a hand up and clenched his
fist as he spoke. "I can tighten my grip over generations
without a single war needing to be fought. People will be
born, live their lives, and pass away all under my watch.
They will learn that my rule is simply the way of things.
It will be Charles Parker's greatest creation – not merely
a clone." He extended both arms as if to embrace the
boys. "He will have created a *god*."

Aaron's mouth hung open in astonishment. "You
have a serious ego problem."

Just then Onslow Winter shoved his way forward,
brandishing one of the Inventory's holographic phones.
His gaze was drawn to the rows of Dev clones, but he
brought it back to his phone.

"Defences have detected two incoming objects. One
parachute, one coming in like a missile!"

The Collector snatched the phone from him. The holo-display showed the two incoming objects as nothing more defined than dots.

"It looks like an ill-advised rescue attempt," sniggered the Collector as one dot speared towards the ground. "If these are your friends, they don't stand a chance."

A deep boom suddenly echoed around the room. Mason ducked, thinking they were under attack from outside before he realized the sound had been from the pipes around the room as they suddenly pumped a blue fluid into the bank of glass cylinders and bubbles began to blast the bodies, making them convulse.

The Collector took a step back in confusion.

"No . . . this isn't possible. . ."

"What's happening?" asked Aaron as he stared at the tanks.

Mason smiled. "I think the cavalry is coming. . ."

LOT'S TURN

Lot's arms flailed as she fought to keep the air-board level. It was a pointless act and she knew it. The board was too aerodynamic so wouldn't slow her down enough . . . but it might buy her precious time.

With nothing left to lose, she snapped her parachute's harness from around her thighs and loosened it around her waist. She tried to rotate the pack around, but with her arms still strapped in, it was impossible.

She had no choice but to do the unthinkable.

She slackened the shoulder straps and slid her arms from the harness. Now she was completely unattached to the parachute and still free-falling. If the wind tore it from her grip now, she would plummet to her death. Even as a thrill seeker, this was too much for Lot.

With every second counting, she forced herself to concentrate on swapping the arm straps, first her left, then her right. Every movement threatened to pull the chute from her sweaty palms. She was moving quickly, but her mind played events in agonizing slow motion.

She managed to rotate the pack on her chest and immediately rushed to tighten the arm straps, then the legs. She pulled them so tight she feared she'd cut off the blood circulation to her limbs – but right now that wasn't her main concern.

Her hands ran across the pack. Thanks to her parents, she knew how the parachute opened – the pilot chute normally is first to go, expanding and pulling out three metres of webbing known as the bridle. The bridle pulls the closing pin free – and that releases the D-bag (or deployment bag) that in turn pulls taut the nylon riser lines that finally slide the main canopy from the container. . .

Lot didn't have any time for that. She snapped the pin free with one hand and used the other to physically yank the D-bag out. The air took it immediately and she learned the valuable lesson of why the main pack was worn on the back. The D-bag smashed her in the face and everything went black.

"That was interesting."

The voice seemed to come from very far away. There was a strong metallic smell and the taste of iron . . . then a white pinpoint of light slowly widened and became blinding. Slowly, Riya came into focus and Lot realized she was lying flat on her back.

Riya was leaning over her, using a broken fence pole as a crutch. Lot sat up and felt pain across every inch of her body.

"I wouldn't do that—" Riya began, reaching to push her back, but Lot was already sitting upright. "Never mind. When do you ever listen to me? If you broke your neck then you're not supposed to move."

Lot rubbed her neck. It was sore, but she could move it. "I don't think I've broken anything."

"Lucky you." Riya nodded to her left leg. She had formed a basic splint by tying a wooden fence slat to her leg with a coil of wire from the same fence. "I have." She indicated to her arm in the cast. "I'm falling apart this whole mission." She circled her finger around her own face. "Although you've got a little blood . . . everywhere."

"The pack hit me in the face. It's better than being dead, I guess. Where are we?" She tried to stand, but her feet were still attached to the air-board, which had broken in half. The rest of her chute was spread out in the mud around her. She tugged the clamps binding her feet and stood up. A wave of dizziness hit her, and Riya caught her.

"We're in a field, as far as I can tell, on Inventory land. The defence system fired flak." Like Riya, she was familiar with the clouds of explosive particles designed to take down enemy missiles. Or, in this case, parachutists. "They must have thought you were a missile, the speed you were going. I think any later and you would have been as flat as a pancake. Maybe flatter."

Lot shook Riya's supporting hand away and looked around. She recognized the lie of the land and indicated to a hill.

"The farm's that way."

Lot began walking towards it. "If they shot at us and didn't come out to inspect the wreckage. . ."

"Then they don't think there were any survivors," Riya finished, hobbling after her. "Yeah. You've been down for the count for about fifteen minutes and nobody's come running. I'd say we're safe . . . for now. As long as we don't trigger any of their alarms, and stay out of camera range. But the problem is, we still can't get in."

"I'm sure we'll think of something."

Riya sat down on a hay bale and winced as pain shot through her broken leg. "That's your plan?"

Lot shrugged. She brushed the hay off the Iron Fist glove, relieved that the Inventory technicians hadn't found it.

"I thought only Dev could use that thing with his freaky power." Riya waggled her fingers like some kind of magician.

"This was built a long time ago when people didn't have freaky powers." She fluttered her fingers, making Riya laugh. "Dev once told me that it has some basic controls anyone should be able to use."

She put her hand inside the gauntlet. Her fingers felt snug inside. She hoisted it up in front of her and made a fist, as she'd seen Dev do so many times.

Nothing happened.

Already her arm was aching from trying to hold the pose. Dev's synaesthesia used to effortlessly communicate with the gauntlet, commanding it to activate. Now she had to find a good old-fashioned start button.

"Impressive," scoffed Riya.

Lot couldn't be sure, but it felt as if the glove was growing tighter around her hand. Something cold was pressing against her fingertips. She experimentally pushed her index finger forward. It felt as if she was pressing a switch.

Hexagonal panels suddenly extended from the gauntlet, smothering her completely. She staggered back in surprise as the Iron Fist mech grew around her: swelling under her feet, raising her to be an imposing eight feet tall.

The panels covered her face, plunging her into darkness for several seconds. Then she heard a high-pitched whine and a display screen suddenly extended in front of her eyes. It was disorienting to look down at Riya.

"Awesome!" Riya shouted, punching the air.

Lot took a few experimental steps in the mech. It effortlessly followed her every movement. She extended her hands and waggled her fingers; the suit moved smoothly.

Riya stood and leaned on her crutch. "You know I'm

not going to be much use. Are you sure you can take them on?"

"I'm going to need—" The suit amplified Lot's voice, transforming it into a deep booming sound. "Wow! I sound awesome!"

Riya coughed for attention.

"Sorry," said Lot. "You know the Inventory security protocols. It will be on lockdown. Even the Collector had trouble getting in the first time. We're going to need to get them to open up willingly."

"And how are we going to do that?" asked Riya, although she already knew the horrible answer to that question.

Riya hollered at the top of her lungs as she threw another brick through the farmhouse window. Glass tinkled across the kitchen table beyond.

"Come on, you cowards! Get out here and fight!"

She hobbled around the front door, searching for another rock. She was aware that dozens of security cameras were tracking her every move and she hoped the Collector thought she was worth punishing.

The faint sound of metal doors sliding open from within the house alerted her that security had indeed been sent from below. Two soldiers stepped out from the house and regarded her with a chuckle. They hadn't even bothered removing their rifles from their shoulders.

"Here we were hoping for a scrap," one said to the other. "And instead there's just some screeching girl."

Riya steadied her balance and raised her crutch like a baseball bat. "Bring it on!"

The two soldiers broke into laughter and slowly unslung their rifles. "This is going to be too easy. Sorry to say, but the boss-man wants you atomized. You don't even make decent target practice."

The chatty soldier casually drew aim at Riya. She stared defiantly at him.

Then the Iron Fist mech lunged from the barn — smashing the wooden walls like matchsticks. In two bounds, Lot was with them. A huge fist punched the man off his feet so hard he sailed across the yard and crashed through a far barn, leaving a guard-shaped hole before he crashed into the hay bales inside. With at least a dozen bones broken, he lay there and gently whimpered in pain.

The second soldier fired at Lot, but the energy pulses bounced from the mech's armour.

Lot snatched the rifle from his hand and effortlessly

snapped it in half. Then she picked the man up and threw him upwards – only for him to come crashing down through the farmhouse roof with a wailing scream.

Without a word, Lot ran into the farmhouse, the broad shoulders of the mech smashing the brickwork around the door. Tables and chairs in the kitchen were crushed as she charged towards the secure elevator leading to the bowels of the Inventory. Already the doors were closing.

Lot reached out, catching them with the mech's powerful fists. She didn't need to strain to push them back open. She stepped into the elevator, crouching so the mech would fit. She knew the Iron Fist security was to stop tech from getting out ... not getting in. To do that she would have to face the Collector's entire team. Things were going to get messy.

The last thing she saw as the doors swished closed was Riya outside whooping with delight and giving Lot a thumbs up.

"Go get them!"

ARMY OF ONE

All the Dev clones were violently jerking in their glass cylinders as the streams of bubbles increased. The liquids changed from blue to amber.

"What exactly is going on?" asked Onslow Winter, his eyes riveted on the spectacle.

"The clones are waking..." said the Collector uncertainly. "They're just empty shells. Useless lumps of flesh..."

"How is that possible?"

The Collector could only shake his head; he was wondering the very same thing. He took a step closer to the nearest tank and wiped the condensation off the glass. The clone inside looked as if it was having a fit.

"Perhaps it's a malfunction, or a self-destruct sequence," Winter suggested.

Then the clone opened its eyes and stared at the Collector. And automated voice on the Eternal Machine suddenly spoke up:

"Developer Clone 303.2 activated."

Aaron and Mason swapped a look of incredulity. "Developer . . . *Dev. . .*"

"Developer Clone 304.2 activated."

The Collector looked around in surprise as the eyes of another clone opened and glared at him. "No . . . that's impossible. . ."

"Developer Clone 304.2 activated. Developer Clone 305.2 deceased. Developer Clone 306.2 activated. . ." The computer was now uttering a stream of activations.

The Collector started to walk back towards the door. Sensing the danger, Winter kept close to his side.

"Developer Clone 323.2 activated."

The room was suddenly filled with the sound of shattering glass as twenty clones punched and kicked their way free, the amniotic fluid splashing across the floor. They snatched up shards of broken cylinder glass to arm themselves. The Collector and Winter were already fleeing from the room with their guards following as the clones were freed.

Mason, Aaron and Norman stared in astonishment as the clones slowly stood and took in the room before finally focusing on Mason.

"Hello, Mase," said twenty Devs in unison.

Mason eventually found his voice. "D-Dev?"

"It's me," they said. "I've just downloaded my brain into . . . all of them."

"That was an awesome idea," said Aaron, staring at each identical clone in turn.

"It was a bit of a mistake, to be honest," said twenty Devs in embarrassment. "I had been aiming for one. And this is giving me a splitting headache already."

"Where . . . are you, the real you?" Mason asked, still trying to get his head around what was happening.

"This is the real me. The old me is probably dead, sitting in a backup Inventory in orbit."

Mason held up his hand to stop him. "Tell me later. First, we'd really like to get out of here."

"Later. Now we have to stop the Collector."

"Yeah? You and whose army?" joked Mason – then looked around at the Devs. "Oh, you already have one. Just one thing, mate," Mason added, lowering his voice.

The nearest Dev leaned closer. "What?"

"Before you go saving the world, you all better go and put some clothes on."

Norman the technician proved to be the minor hero of the hour. He admitted to having been to this zone numerous times previously with Charles Parker, like the other technicians involved with the Eternal Machine. Leading them all back to the chamber with the three cryo-pods, he had revealed the mystery of the second door: it led to a changing room with more than enough identical clothing for the clones. He was also able to provide lengths of piping, saws, hammers and anything else that could be used as a weapon.

Mason and Aaron were still reeling from the bizarre sight of a score of Devs hurrying silently around. He had so many questions to ask, he just didn't know which one to approach. Instead, Mason slipped away and examined the cryo-pods.

Fully clothed, the Devs followed Normal down the corridor, only to find that the Collector had demolished the entrance to trap them inside. Norman, as usual, was unperturbed. He led them back to the junction in the corridor and took the only other corridor.

Aaron and Mason followed, the army of Devs behind. The corridor continued sloping downward and they walked in silence for a minute before a Dev caught up with them.

"Guys," the Dev said, rubbing his temple in concentration. The other clones hadn't spoken.

"Do you know how weird this is?" Mason whispered back, although he wasn't sure why he didn't want the other Devs to overhear. "It's freaking me out."

Dev chuckled. "Freaking you out? It's really difficult to focus on just one. . ." He indicated to his body. "I don't think the machine was designed to be spread over multiple clones. My head is killing me, and I feel thin . . . like rubber about to snap."

"Thanks for the rescue attempt," Aaron said. "But we're still stuck here."

"Not stuck. We have the Collector on the run. He's trapped in here. He can't get the tech out without me. Us. And if he sets foot outside, the World Consortium and the Company will come crashing down on him." At least twelve of him hoped that was the case.

Mason felt a brief glimmer of hope. "You've heard from the sarge?"

Dev shook his head. "Wade is ... gone. The Company are the only force left."

Mason stopped in his tracks, his legs trembling. The news of Sergeant Wade had struck him hard. He'd always liked her and harboured a secret suspicion that she was related to Dev in some way. Once, after they had discovered Dev was a clone, he and Lot had speculated that she could even have been Dev's mother...

A flicker of sorrow rippled across the Devs' faces. "We don't have time."

Mason nodded and continued walking.

"Here we are," said Norman, indicating the party should stop.

"Where is here, exactly?" Dev asked.

Norman wagged a finger at a door ahead. "The only other way out."

"Where does it go?"

Norman shook his head, then hazarded a guess. "Probably the lowest point of the Inventory; the most secure. And the Collector is under attack. He would retire to the safest place too."

Dev nodded in understanding and placed his hand

on the secure keypad. He licked his lips as he focused his synaesthesia to unlock the door. Another migraine pain shot through his skull. It was difficult to control so many clones and the power at the same time.

He pulled himself together and focused. The end was in sight. . .

He just hoped his army was up for the task.

MOMENTUM

Lot was surprised by how little resistance she encountered as she powered through the corridors. Three of the Collector's soldiers had been waiting at the bottom of the elevator. Their laser blasts had been powerful enough to knock her off her feet, but the mech's armour deflected the shots – two into the ceiling, and the third rebounded to strike the man who had fired it.

Lot had pressed a couple of buttons inside the gauntlet, hoping to activate the weapons, but nothing happened. Instead she backhanded one soldier into the wall, and the other was punched so hard he vanished down the corridor without hitting the floor.

Audible hammering from the other side of the canteen door rose her hope that her friends were inside. Using the mech's enhanced strength, she heaved the door open and saw the room was full of Inventory staff. All the technicians and scientists crammed inside were relieved to see her. As one they began cheering and chanting:

"Dev! Dev! Dev!"

"I'm not. . ." Lot began, but the mech's booming voice sounded the same whether it was her or Dev speaking. She didn't have time to correct them.

Lot sprinted into the Green Zone. With every step, she was getting used to the mech and could see why Dev loved using it. She only regretted that she didn't have the rocket-pack attachments. That would have been a whole new level of fun.

More laser bolts slammed into her as she emerged from the first set of shelves in the Green Zone. A dozen soldiers had been waiting to ambush her. A couple of laser bolts were one thing, but a sustained hail of fire was causing damage. She raised her arm to protect her head and crouched to make herself a smaller target. Black singe marks pocked the suit. Inside, alarms started to sound and a schematic of the suit flashed up on her display, highlighting the damaged areas.

Five soldiers knelt three storeys up on a huge shelving unit filled with a variety of helicopter-like vehicles that made a perfect shield to hide behind.

With a snarl, Lot jumped to the base of the shelf and strained to topple it. At first it didn't move, and the warning alarms in Lot's helmet indicated the servomotors that gave her enhanced strength were on the verge of burning out.

The men on the shelves scrambled towards the edge so they could shoot down on her. Then the shelf started to creak. Lot put her shoulder into it — and the entire shelving unit slowly began to topple. The steel twisted as the front of the shelves fell, the contents of men and machines cascading off with a thunderous roar. Like an undulating snake, the shelving stretching down the Inventory also began to crash to the floor.

Lot's victory was short-lived as the remaining seven soldiers circled behind her, opening fire as they ran. Lot snatched a fallen helicopter by the tail and spun it around before releasing it like an Olympic hammer-thrower.

The aircraft smashed into four of the soldiers, the rotors and tail snapping off and narrowly missing the others. Unwilling to continue being target practice, Lot ran across the open floor towards Eema's husk. She didn't know what had happened to the old robot, but she had a fitting send-off for her old guardian.

With more alarms bleeping in her suit, Lot raised the huge spherical hulk above her head. With a bellow, she hurled it at the four soldiers. In horror, they turned their laser fire on to the rolling hulk. Chunks of Eema's panelling were blasted off, but it did nothing to stop Eema from bowling into them like skittles.

"STRIKE!" Lot yelled triumphantly, then realized that nobody was around to see her victory. "Well, my boys won't save themselves," she muttered to herself. With a sigh, she continued further into the Inventory. "I'm on my way..."

She just hoped they were still alive.

The door opened inwards with a gentle hiss.

Dev motioned for the others to stay back, a mostly useless gesture since nineteen of them were himself. Peering into the room beyond, he recognized it instantly.

"We're in the Red Zone," he whispered to Mason.

It made sense that the Black Zone connected directly here, as this was the most secure part of the inventory, where the original cloning labs were located. From his position, Dev could see several blast doors in the far wall, covering the rooms beyond in which he had been created. Or at least his body had, he corrected himself – as far as he knew, his mind was unique.

He became aware of voices on the far side of the chamber. Flickering energy cubes displayed a shifting wall of dots, like an animated Magic Eye picture. These housed the most precious artefacts in the collection. If Dev focused his eyes correctly, the dots would merge together so he could see and touch the device.

The scattered display cubes also prevented him from seeing who else was in the room, yet one voice was all too familiar.

"Deal with it!" the Collector snapped.

Onslow Winter spoke up. "She's already through the Blue Zone—"

"It's one girl! How hard can that be?"

Devs' hearts skipped a beat. One stubborn girl causing trouble – he guessed who that would be.

He heard the far door hiss closed and the sound of the Collector walking across the room. Dev didn't need to communicate his idea to his clone;, they all had it at exactly the same time. The Devs filed silently past

Mason and Aaron, the last one turning to Mason and patting him on the shoulder.

"You guys wait here. We've got this."

The surprise on the Collector's face was unmistakable when Dev stepped out from behind a pulsing display case.

"Dev?" The fiend composed himself. "You always seem to turn up at the most inopportune times."

"I get everywhere." With that, his clones stepped into view, completely circling the Collector.

The Collector turned a full 360 degrees. "So I see. Like a bad rash, you keep multiplying. This is not going to get you anywhere. I already have everything I need. Strike me down and I will rise again ... and again ... and again..."

"And I will stop you each time."

"No, Dev. Your, huh, development stops here. You –" he gestured to the clones "– are the last of your kind. You think you know me. You think you can anticipate my every move. But you can't. I have always been a dozen steps ahead. It is the twisted thinking I inherited from our father. I always win, even when you perceive I am losing."

He gestured with his hand to a blast shield on the

wall. It opened, revealing a large window, and the cloning lab beyond.

"Our genetic codes were created in there. I have already removed my samples, ready for a rebirth."

Then, with a slight tilt of his head, an explosive device that had been pre-laid in the room detonated. The reinforced windows shattered outward as a fierce orange fireball incinerated the room.

The Collector smiled. "I left yours inside." He gestured to the Devs. "You are all suddenly an endangered species. There is no coming back from this."

"There's twenty of me. All willing to fight to the death. There is only one of you."

The Collector sighed and raised his hands.

The Devs didn't move; he knew a trap when he saw it. The Collector smiled and lowered his hands.

"Very good. Like I said, I am always ahead of you."

The Devs gasped when the blast door shield protecting another lab opened, revealing one of the Collector's loyal soldiers holding what looked like an electric cattle prod in one hand, which hovered threateningly next to—

"Wade! You're alive!"

JUST A GIRL

The hull of the battleship reverberated like a gong as the stream of bio-bots whipped against it. In the battle mech, Lot rolled aside — narrowly missing the strike. The huge ship was suspended on massive trellises in the Blue Zone's dry dock, home to the collection's range of aquatic inventions.

Lot had been sprinting through the Zone when Onslow Winter had emerged from the Red Zone. She had been shocked and surprised to see him and had wanted to ask if Sergeant Wade was still with him ... but any concept that he was an ally vanished before she could open her mouth. Bio-bot tentacles had rippled from his shoulders and flailed at her.

She'd just dodged aside in time to see more bio-bots emerge from the man's skin, covering his body in a protective shield, forming the featureless humanoid shape that was the Winter Storm. Like her mech suit, the bio-bots boosted Onslow's physique, making him taller and more muscular until he was the same size as the mech.

The two giants faced one another.

"There are reinforcements coming," Lot warned him. "There is no way you escape from here. Give up before you get hurt."

"Too late for that." Six long tentacles erupted from his shoulders and back, and Winter lashed out, hitting the ship as Lot rolled aside. "My bio-bots are the only things keeping me alive."

"We can help you!"

"The Collector already has." He lashed out again, forcing Lot to roll under the keel of the immense battleship. "And he can fix me. Give me eternal life."

"Trust me. That's not how he works. Once he has no further use of you, it's game over."

"No," growled Winter, "it's over for you."

He stomped the ground hard, sending cracks running through the concrete floor. More bio-bots poured from him with an increasingly loud buzz, like a swarm of killer bees. They swirled in a furious whirlwind before striking at Lot.

She ducked, dodging it just in time, and it smashed into the trellis instead. But a few of the swarm caught the side of the mech's head with such force they tore a chunk from her helmet, breaking open her view. At least it stopped the nagging alarms.

But Lot hadn't been the bio-bots' target. The furious swarm sliced through the trellis as if it were plasticine. The metal bubbled and buckled – then gave way under the 58,000 tons of battleship that it was holding up. With a mighty squeal, the battleship's prow fell several metres, smashing a crater in the floor. The ship's own weight buckled the entire keel, twisting the ship out of shape. Rivets popped and steel panels cracked as the entire ship began to capsize towards Lot.

She ran, the mech's feet slipping on the smooth floor. The battleship was so huge it looked as if it was falling in slow motion. The shadow of the immense hull rolled over Lot—

With a final bound she *just* made it clear as the ship crashed on to its side with a deafening boom that echoed through the Blue Zone like rolling thunder.

Lot fell face first on the ground and caught her breath. The movements of the damaged mech were sluggish and the display screen flickered within her helmet, forcing her to peer through the crack to see properly.

The echo still reverberated around the warehouse as Winter Storm clambered on to the side of the stricken battleship, carried by the six bio-bot tentacles that suspended him in the air a metre off the ground.

"Is this how you imagined your end to be," he jeered, "killed in a pathetic, hapless rescue attempt? You're a child. You never stood a chance."

The anger that surged through Lot flushed away the fear she had been feeling just moments before. With complete clarity, she knew exactly what to do.

From her crouched position, Lot broke into a sprint. The malfunctioning mech suit felt as if she was running through mud, but she pressed on with every ounce of strength she possessed. The door back into the Green Zone was just ahead.

Onslow Winter's laughter taunted her from behind. "And now you run like a coward. You're such a disappointment, Lottie."

He scuttled down the side of the battleship like a

malformed insect. By the time he was on the ground, Lot was already in the Green Zone. She wildly punched the door lock as she passed through, and the great reinforced shutters began to slide closed. She didn't pause to look behind as she ran.

She didn't see the bio-bot tentacle narrowly thrust through the decreasing gap to prevent the doors from locking. More bio-bots flooded into the gap and pushed back. With the strain of metal, the powerful motors sealing the door ground to a stop – then were forced into reverse as the bots drew the door open wide enough for Winter Storm to stride through.

There was no sign of Lot in the Green Zone. Winter paused to listen ... then slowly advanced towards the nearest aisle.

"There is no escape. You shouldn't have come."

He leapt into an aisle, expecting to see Lot cowering in her broken mech. But there was nobody. He slowly turned around, searching for the most likely hidey-hole; there was no way she had time to leave the Zone.

"Come out, come out wherever you are," he sang.

"Oh, I'm right here," said Lot from above him.

Winter Storm looked up to see Lot was standing on a shelf a storey above him. This particular shelf was filled with exotic engines and generators that had been confiscated throughout the years. Her suit was sparking, covered in black scorch marks, and he could see her eye peering at him through the crack in the helmet.

"And I'm not hiding," she said in a sing-song voice. "I'm a-hunting. . ."

She raised her arm, and Winter saw one of the engines was attached to it. The mech had the ability to bond gadgets into its frame, using them to further the suit's abilities. Dev had often used a pair of rocket packs attached to his back. Lot had remembered this engine strapped to her arm from several months back when she had watched the Inventory technicians experiment with it – and felt inspired after watching how the cyclone in Bangladesh had affected Winter Storm.

She jumped down, the mech buzzing in distress as it absorbed the landing. "A-hunting with my hurricane," she added – then powered up the engine by pushing two of the finger controls in her gauntlet – just as Winter Storm rose his six bio-bot tentacles over his head like a scorpion's stinger.

"Divide and conquer," Lot growled as the Hurricane engine fired.

A single puff of air shot from the engine and into

Winter Storm. A single puff that within it packed the punch of a hurricane, a storm to end the Winter Storm. So close that the punch blew every single bio-bot off Onslow Winter, scattering them across the warehouse. The bots were living things, and nothing alive could withstand the hurricane. Dispersed to individual microscopic components spread out across the room, the surviving bots were unable to re-form so instead lay uselessly on their own. The swarm had been defeated.

Onslow Winter was pitched down an aisle – sailing through the air for almost a kilometre before slamming into the distant shelves. Lot was somewhat annoyed that he was too far to hear the quip she had been rehearsing in her head.

"Winter's over, and it's time for spring."

OK, it had sounded better in her head.

TWENTY TO ONE

From his hiding place, Mason hissed with distress as the soldier ushered Sergeant Wade from the lab and into the Red Zone, the prod dangerously close to her head.

"That is an Evaporation Stick," the Collector explained. "One touch and every drop of moisture in her body will—" He made a *puff* sound and flicked his fingers to show how she would become dust. "And if you don't surrender, that's exactly what will happen."

"And if we do surrender . . . you'll do it anyway," said a Dev.

Mason whispered to Aaron. "We have to do something!"

"Other than provide target practice?" Other than a few blunt tools in a box, he could find nothing immediately useful.

"We're in a room full of deadly tech. There must be something we can use!"

Mason motioned to stand, but technician Norman placed a hand on his shoulder to stop him. "Remember, this is the Red Zone. There are things in here that could destroy the world. None of these will merely destroy the room."

"You're saying this stuff is too dangerous to use?" said Mason in despair. Norman nodded. Mason rubbed his head – how was it possible he was surrounded by so many weapons which were all useless?

Or maybe not. . .

"So we have reached a stalemate?" said the Collector to the Devs arced around him, armed with an assortment of weapons more at home in a garden centre. "Congratulations. You are almost as devious as me."

The soldier brought Wade up to him.

She looked at Dev with wide eyes. "I'm sorry, Dev. There was nothing I could do. We brought Onslow Winter here. . ."

"Enough!" snapped the Collector. "This is not

the time for reunions. Especially ones that will be so unfortunately short-lived."

"I don't think so!" bellowed Mason as he strode into the room with Aaron by his side. He held aloft a white spherical object that he had taken from a display cube. "Let her go, or I will detonate this!"

The Collector looked genuinely surprised to see him. "My gosh. It looks like the whole gang has come home. Father would be pleased." He pointed at the sphere. "Do you have any idea what that is?"

Mason smiled smugly. "Oh yeah. A Higgs-Bos-Bomb. I read the label and I ain't afraid to use it."

"Do you know what it does?"

Mason flashed his best maniacal smile. "No. Nobody does! Shall we find out?" His thumb hovered over the single recessed button on the device.

"STOP!" The Collector gestured to his soldier. "Let her go."

The soldier lowered the prod and shoved Wade forward. She gratefully ran through the line of Devs and joined Mason and Aaron.

"I'm so happy to see you," Mason said, patting her on the arm.

"You too," she said, her eyes never leaving the Higgs-

Bos-Bomb. "I don't want to sound all Parker-like, but maybe I can..."

Mason handed the bomb to her. "Sure. I'd rather not be carrying something that could potentially destroy the universe. Knowing my luck..."

"You always have bad luck, Mason." She gingerly took the sphere from him.

"Tell me about it."

"Or I'll show you."

Wade's odd comment didn't register until it was too late. Wade moved her hand close to his face, and he could see the nozzle of the dimensionalizer pointed at him.

"Wwhhhaaat?" he wailed.

All the Devs looked around in confusion.

Wade threw a little wave at him. "All this time as a sleeper agent has really been a drag. Helping Shadow Helix break in here the first time. Making sure I covered their tracks so you couldn't easily find them when they escaped." She shook her head. "And then, just when I thought I could walk away from all of this, the World Consortium go and put me in charge! We didn't expect that, did we?"

"It was a pleasant surprise," said the Collector.

"Then making sure you found Wan-Soo as the mole, well, that was a chore, let me tell you."

Dev exchanged glances with himselves. He'd always known there was something wrong that day on-board the oil rig when Wan-Soo had been revealed as a traitor, shortly before he died.

Wade continued. "Setting up everything with Onslow Winter to get in here took precision planning. And now, this close to achieving everything, you all turn up and try to throw a spanner in the works. That's just not fair."

The Collector addressed the nearest clone. "You see, Dev? *Always* a step ahead. Winter Storm is dealing with that pain of a girlfriend of yours, and Wade has a twitchy trigger finger. I have planned for every eventually."

"Not every. . ."

Dev enjoyed the second look of surprise that crossed the Collector's face as Norman stepped from his hiding place and approached Wade.

"You see, I am an old hand here. I have seen you created from nothing." He wagged a finger at the Collector. "You have eyes that can see through people; see wavelengths we can only imagine; see deep into the heart of the cosmos. But I have seen inventions and ingenuity that defies the imagination." He gestured to Mason, Aaron and Dev, his eyes brimming with tears. "Ah, and my Scavengers. With you I have seen unquestionable bravery." He looked defiantly at the Collector. "And what you didn't see . . . was a distraction."

For an old man, he moved with considerable speed. He threw something to Aaron before Wade, who had switched the dimensionalizer from Mason to Norman, fired. A cloud of nanoparticles sprayed over Norman and he screamed as he suddenly shifted from a solid three dimensions to two: less than an atom thick. Without any depth to balance him, Norman flopped backwards and shattered like a mirror as he hit the floor.

At the same moment, Aaron had deftly caught the wrench Norman had thrown him. Using all his strength, he clobbered Wade across the back of the head. As Norman's body shattered into oblivion, Wade collapsed unconscious to the floor. Mason flinched as the Higgs-Bos-Bomb bounced on the floor and rolled away.

"NNNOOO!!" roared the Collector, lashing out at the nearest Dev.

The Devs moved with flawless coordination. Three

leapt on the solider who struck one with the Evaporation Stick. The clone burst into dust. The soldier staggered under the weight of the other two – jabbing one in the ribs and evaporating him.

The third Dev managed to knock the stick from his hand and wrestled with him on the floor.

Meanwhile, the remaining sixteen Devs mobbed the Collector with their ragtag collection of weapons. A firm shoulder knocked two Devs into the nearby display case. There was a flash, and the clones were vaporized on impact.

The Collector went down under the weight of the fourteen Devs who piled on him like a rugby scrum.

Mason and Aaron could do nothing to help, so instead used their belts to bind Wade's hands and feet after first taking the dimensionalizer from her

With a furious bellow, the Collector sprang to his feet with every ounce of strength he possessed. The Devs were cast aside, another three disintegrating against the storage cubes.

Three Devs surrounded the Collector, armed with a metal pipe, sledgehammer and, bizarrely, a gun one of the clones had snagged along the way. The Dev had thought it would be a lethal weapon, but it turned out to be a laundry gun, designed to clean clothes while still worn. He had only discovered this while shooting one of the soldiers moments ago. Instead of incapacitating the man, it had left him with freshly laundered uniform. The solider was at least shocked long enough for another Dev to whack him unconscious with a shovel.

The other eight Devs kept back and watched.

The exertion had left the Collector gasping for breath. "Is this how you think it should end? Brother against brother?"

"You're not my brother," said the Devs. "You're just a failed science project."

With a wild scream, the Collector lunged at one of the Devs — tackling him to the floor. Without any weapon or gadget, Dev on his own was physically no match for the Collector, who whaled a volley of punches on him, breaking his nose, before the closest two Devs could catch up.

More Devs moved in to drag the Collector away, pinning him down and clambering on top of him. The battered Dev stood up and wiped his bloodied nose.

"What will it take to stop you?"

Again, the Collector kicked and shoved the pile of Devs off him, but this time he didn't try to run. Instead he held up something in his hand: the Higgs-Bos-Bomb. He had been deliberately making his way to the discarded weapon.

"We are both freaks of nature, Dev. We belong dead."

He thumbed the detonator.

Every Dev bellowed for him to stop. A Dev jumped at Mason and Aaron, the others piling on to the Collector in an attempt to contain the blast.

The Higgs-Bos-Bomb detonated.

Mason was shoved in the face by a Dev pushing him to the ground. He heard a low bass hum from the detonation – a hum that dropped so low it shook his guts.

The Higgs boson was a fundamental quantum particle responsible for giving everything mass. The detonation released a flood of particles – which, due to their short-lived nature, didn't manage to travel very far. They encompassed the Collector and the Devs wrestling him – and they all became super-heavy. Every atom in their bodies suddenly crunched to the ground as if they were melting at high speed. In less than the blink of an eye they all vanished – the Devs and the Collector – broken into subatomic bits that bounced harmlessly off the floor.

Only when silence reigned did Mason open his eyes.

The Dev on top of him had been half caught in the blast of particles, and only his hand remained lying on the floor. Aaron stirred next to him and they both slowly stood up to inspect the damage.

There was none.

The display cases were intact and, other than a hemispherical dent in the floor where the bomb had touched the concrete, there was no sign anything had happened.

With a jaded sound of servomotors, Lot came running into the room, stopping when she saw Mason's shocked expression.

"He's gone. . ." muttered Mason.

"Thank god for that!" cried Aaron.

Mason's frown deepened. "I meant Dev, not the Collector."

"Oh . . . OH!" said Aaron, twisting around as he noted the clones had all been destroyed.

With a *schnikt* of metal plates peeling away, Lot deactivated the mech and let the gauntlet slide off her hand. It fell with a heavy thud, smoke drifting from it.

Lot took a faltering step towards her friends. "Dev. . .?"

Mason had tears in his eyes as he shook his head. Lot gave a sharp intake of breath, but surprised herself when she failed to cry. She hugged Mason tightly. It seemed the only thing to do to mark their loss.

"What's going on?"

"Dev..." sobbed Mason. "We've lost ... Dev?" He suddenly looked up. "DEV?!"

Still nursing his busted nose, Dev staggered from between the display cases. Lot gave a bark of laughter — and *now* tears rolled down her cheeks. She crossed to Dev, who held out his arms in anticipation of a hug.

Lot slapped him hard across the cheek.

"That's for what you did to me!"

Dev was unsure if she meant the kiss or having her knocked unconscious. He thought it best not to ask.

REUNITED

With the Inventory no longer under siege, the crew Lot had freed from the canteen soon had everything back up and running. The first thing Dev insisted on was sending a communication to Fabian at the Company to check on his uncle. Lot and Riya had expected him to be furious with them, but when Fabian appeared on the screen in the control bunker, he looked worn and tired.

"It pleases me to see you all alive."

"You look it," Lot said sarcastically.

Fabian paused, trying to find the right words.

"Devon. Your uncle passed away. I'm sorry."

Dev was dumbstruck. After all the recent losses, this

was almost too much to bear. The others bowed their heads in grief.

"We tried our best to keep him alive. If it's any consolation, we uploaded his memories in a TelePath. I'd like to give it to you as a token of goodwill between our agencies."

Lot squeezed Dev's shoulder in sympathy.

"You downloaded his brain?" said Mason almost cheerfully.

"Well, not quite; just his memories, like Professor Lu did," Fabian said, perplexed by Mason's sudden jovial mood.

"Awesome! How fast can you get here?"

"What're you—"

Mason spun Dev around, his eyes wide with delight. "This is going to sound weird – wait, no, it's not. Around here, this is going to sound perfectly normal. But I've got a plan!"

Fabian joined them a few hours later. He tried to act sombre in light of Charles Parker's death, but as a Company man setting foot into the Inventory for the first time, he was buzzing with excitement.

Mason led the party down to the Black Zone, where

a knot of technicians was waiting around the two occupied cryo-pods. Mason drew Fabian's attention to the empty one.

"This is where a pal of yours slept."

Fabian's eyes went round when he read the name plate. "Stephan!"

Mason smiled when he saw Dev was still baffled. "For once, I have got the jump on you, mate. And it feels good!" He gave a little jig, prolonging his moment of smugness.

"Mase . . . just tell me. . ."

"OK. When Stephan — I mean, Tyker — came here, your uncle didn't want to see him."

"That's right. He didn't want to trigger any memories. . ." Tyker and Charles had worked closely together in the past.

"Yeeeaaah," said Mason, elongating the word to show it wasn't the full answer. "But also, they were pals. Best friends, in fact. And your uncle didn't want to look at his old friend only to be reminded that *he* had aged, but Tyker hadn't."

"How do you know that?" Lot asked sceptically.

"Because I listen. Well, not *listen* exactly . . . but I remember a few odd things Tyker said, and I'm putting it all together. Like a detective!"

Dev rubbed his head. Since the clones had all been destroyed, his headache had eased and he didn't feel as *stretched*, but he still felt weak and emotionally drained. "I don't know why you're telling me this."

Mason gave a theatrical sigh and looked at all the confused faces around him. "Am I the only one getting this?" Everybody's blank looks confirmed he was. "Wow, really? This is the greatest moment of my life. I am officially the smartest person in the Inventory. I—"

"Mase!" snapped Riya impatiently. She raised one of her crutches, given to her by the medical staff, and poked Mason in the ribs. "Get to the point."

Mason wiped the condensation from the cryo-pod next to him. Inside was a middle-aged man with jet-black hair.

"Meet your uncle."

Dev recognized the face from when he had been carrying Tyker's memories. It was his uncle, preserved in a much younger state.

"He cloned himself!" gasped Fabian.

"Bingo!" yelled Mason. "I bet it was the first experiment he did. Cloning himself to check it was safe, before he made you and all your funky brothers." He playfully nudged Dev, then handed him the TelePath

Fabian had brought along. "We can wake him and give him all his memories back. He's going to be thirty years younger but a heck of a lot wiser."

Dev looked at Mason incredulously. "How did you figure this out?"

Mason straightened to his full height and was about to explain – when Aaron chimed in.

"When you and your clones were getting dressed, he slipped out here and poked around. I saw him. He was accessing that computer to find out what was going on." Aaron pointed to a terminal in the wall.

"Shut up!" huffed Mason, disappointed his moment in the spotlight had been shot down. "And you look stupid with that white hair. . ."

Riya mussed Aaron's hair. "I think it looks kinda cute."

Dev tapped Mason on the chest. "That was still great thinking, mate."

Mason pulled himself together. "Yeah? Well, he is sort of your dad, right?" Dev nodded. Mason moved to the second cryo-pod. "Which means this is kinda your mum."

Dev felt paralyzed as the words sank in. Then he carefully wiped the condensation away. He had seen the woman underneath when he had first entered the Black Zone with Tyker and Lot, but now there was something familiar about her.

As the condensation began covering the glass again, her features became softer, distorted by the moisture. Just like he had seen in Charles Parker's dream. . .

This *was* his wife. This was the mother Dev had never had, nor knew.

Suspended under ice was Dev's family.

Lot squeezed his hand.

"I think it's time we wake them up," she whispered in his ear.